The
Mysterious
Beach Hut

Jacky Atkins

Eloquent Books

Eloquent Books
An imprint of Strategic Book Group
P.O. Box 333
Durham CT 06422
www.StrategicBookGroup.com

ISBN: 978-1-60911-071-0

Printed in the United States of America

To Lucy and Annie and the real little girl

who played on the beach so long ago.

1

There was a gentle knock on the wooden door of the beach hut.

"Please hurry up, I'm freezing out here!"

Holly and Beth looked at each other.

"Who's that?" whispered Beth, hugging her brightly coloured towel round her. She was nine years old and already a good swimmer. There had been some fine waves that afternoon, and she and her sister, Holly, who was three years older, had stayed in the sea for quite a long time. It was a lovely sunny day, but when they came out of the water, the wind felt cold and they'd hurried to the beach hut to warm up.

Holly was already dressed and was sitting on one of the yellow painted box benches running along two sides of the wooden walls. She put down the packet of Jaffa Cakes she had started to open and stood up.

"I don't know, but we'd better find out. She's probably got the wrong beach hut. There's another one with red painted doors just like ours that's farther along."

She opened the door, and the sunlight streamed in. A little girl was standing there, her small fist raised for a second knock. She looked about the same age as Beth. Her light brown hair hung in wet, wavy strands. She was wearing a navy blue swimsuit with small sleeves and a white belt round the waist. It appeared to be made of some kind of woollen material and was quite unlike the swimsuits Holly and Beth wore. But then there were a lot of unusual fashions in Brighton.

"Oh thank you," she said, "I'm so cold, my teeth are chattering. Listen!" She jumped on to the low step into the beach hut with both feet and then reached up to pull down a cream towel with coloured stripes at either end, which was hanging on a nail just inside the door. "Wasn't I silly to leave my towel inside? Mother's always saying, 'Oh, you silly girl, you've forgotten your towel again.'" She laughed and began to dry herself briskly, pulling the towel over her shoulders, round her waist and legs and finally wrapping it round herself like Beth had done. "Are you Josh's friends?" she said. "He told me there were some other girls coming. Josh is my cousin, you know. He lives here. I live in London, but Mother and I are visiting. Daddy's at business, so we came on the train with one of my other cousins and her mother. Do you live here?" The little girl sat down on the box bench and wriggled her toes on the coir matting. "Just getting the sand out," she said.

Holly caught her sister's eye. "Do you know her?" she mouthed silently. Beth shook her head.

"Yes," Holly said, "we do live here, but I don't think we actually know Josh. Are you sure this is, well, what I mean is, you must have come to the wrong beach hut because this one's been ours for years and years. There's another one that's…"

"'COURSE it's the right beach hut!" The little girl laughed. "My towel was in here, and there's my frock." She pointed to a navy dress with a pleated skirt and white stripes round the hem hanging from a hook on the right hand wall. "I know what you're thinking—it almost matches my bathing costume. Mother made it; she likes navy blue. She makes most of my clothes."

The little girl was certainly friendly and seemed quite sure she was in her own beach hut. But why had Holly and Beth not noticed the dress hanging there on the hook? Or the cream beach towel with the coloured stripes? It was all very odd.

"My name's Marjorie, by the way. You must know Josh. Everyone in Brighton knows Josh. Well, a lot of people, anyway. His daddy owns a hotel on the seafront. Oh, I've done it again, I am silly; of course, you probably know him by his real name. That's Morris. We all call him Josh because when he was a baby, his mother—that's my Auntie Hettie; do you know Auntie Hettie?" Holly and Beth shook their heads. "Oh. Well, anyway, Mother says that when Josh was a baby, Auntie Hettie heard a song at the Music Hall about a boy called Josh. She kept on singing it and started to call Morris Josh. It's just his nickname, but it stuck."

Music Hall? Whatever is a music hall? Holly had never heard of such a thing, and she didn't know any of these people Marjorie was talking about. Of course, there had to be some kind of explanation. Maybe Mum knew them, but she'd never said anything about a friend coming this afternoon. It was a complete mystery.

"We don't know a—" began Beth, but Holly gave her a kick under the little table between the bench seats. She wanted to find out more about their strange visitor and her family; it was far too early to end the mystery now.

"Actually, we do know *a* Morris," interrupted Holly. "He was at my last school. Oh, and I'm Holly, Holly Randall, and this is my sister, Beth. We'll ask Mummy about Morris when she comes back. She went to the cafe to get us some tea. We usually make tea here," Holly patted the camping stove on the table, "but the gas bottle for the hob has just run out. She won't be long. I'm sure she'll want to get you some tea too when she sees you're here. Have a Jaffa Cake."

Holly passed the opened packet to Marjorie who removed one carefully from its cellophane bag, looking at it with great interest. She took a little bite, then a bigger one.

"This is lovely!" she said. "I've never had a biscuit like this before. Mother usually buys a bag of mixed ones from the grocer's. Sometimes she lets me choose them. I look through all the glass lids of the big Huntley and Palmer's tins first and then decide. But we only get chocolate ones for special times like birthdays. Is it your birthday?"

"No, but Mummy got those on special offer," said Beth. "Two packets for the price of one. We don't know anywhere where they sell biscuits from tins, do we, Holly? Oh, I know. There're some in that old shop in the museum, but you can't *buy* those."

Marjorie looked mystified, but asked very politely, "Do you think I could possibly have another one? They're *so* lovely!"

The girls ate together for a few moments in companionable silence. They had shut the doors of the beach hut to keep warm, but the sun was streaming though the cracks and under the door.

Holly said, "Let's open the doors now we're warmer. I'll see if Mum's coming."

They all stepped out into the sunlight. The wind had dropped considerably, and the surface of the sea seemed to be covered in dancing lights. A small boat with a red sail was bobbing lazily in the mid-distance, and a dog barked as it chased a gull wheeling low overhead. There was the gentle murmur of water lapping against the groynes which, low down on the beach, were covered with a soft blanket of seaweed. The tide was so low that there was a good expanse of sand below the shingle, and a group of children were playing with a ball at the sea's edge, laughing and calling to each other.

It struck Holly that there was something unusual about the scene. Something had changed. The light was different. Just for a moment, it felt as if they were looking at a heat mirage when the bottom of the picture you see becomes slightly wavy and hazy. It was almost as if, for a split second, time had stood still.

But the moment soon passed. "There they are!" shouted Marjorie happily, and she began to run along the prom, her towel streaming behind her.

Holly and Beth stood watching as she ran in the direction of the old West Pier, its flags barely fluttering in the gentle breeze. It was very quiet; all they could hear was the sound of children's voices, which seemed to be coming from the beach, and some music a long way off like an organ played by a big carousel at a fairground. Only the faintest rumble of traffic came from the usually busy road that ran along the seafront.

Suddenly, Holly froze and took Beth's hand.

"I think we're dreaming. Could we both be dreaming together? What are those flags doing on the old pier? And look! There are people on it! Look at those children and dogs, and people sitting on deck chairs! And over there, can you see there are kiosks with people selling things?"

"And you can get right on to the pier from the prom; it's all been mended and painted! Why didn't we notice this morning?" Beth sounded quite excited. "When Mummy gets back, we must go on it. She'll love it."

Holly looked worried. "We didn't notice it this morning because it wasn't like that. It was still old and broken, and you could only get onto it by the narrow gangway and then only if you were with a special party or doing repairs. Why is the tide so low? When we came out of the sea, it was really high. Don't you remember, the waves were landing us on the shingle? Mummy and I had to put on our flip-flops. You never mind the stones, but you must remember them. We couldn't have been more than ten minutes back in the beach hut when Marjorie knocked on the door. And where's all the traffic gone? There's usually loads at this time of the day, especially when it's so sunny and warm. It's really weird."

"Don't say that; you're scaring me. I want to find Mummy."

"Perhaps we can't. Perhaps—"

Before Holly could go any further, Marjorie was back. Her towel had gone, and she was wearing a dark red knitted jacket over her swimsuit. She grabbed Beth's hand, and then Holly's.

"Come on," she said, "Mother wants to meet you. So does Dulcie, my cousin. Josh and some of the big boys are playing trenches on the beach, and we've got to be the ball boys. Do you know how to play? I'll show you if you don't."

"We can't come because Mummy won't know where we are," Beth objected, almost in tears. Holly put her arm round her.

"No, it's okay, Beth, really it is. The tea place is in this direction. We'll see her coming. She said she'd come along the prom, not past the putting green. And anyway," she added in a quiet whisper to Beth, "we must be dreaming, so it doesn't matter. Let's just have an adventure. We'll wake up any minute and then it will all be gone."

Marjorie's mother had very blue eyes and light brown hair, like her daughter but piled up on top of her head. She wore a high-necked white blouse and a long print skirt. She held out her hand to Holly and then Beth.

"How do you do? Marjorie was just telling me about you. I'm so pleased to see she has made some new friends. If your mother agrees, do come and join our party on the beach."

A little dog was running along beside Marjorie.

"This is Peter," she said. "He's my dog. Mother and Daddy bought him for me. Isn't he lovely?" Marjorie leaned down and put her arms round the little terrier's neck. "When Mother says 'party,' she doesn't mean the hateful sort when you have to wear your best starched frock and eat jellies. I think jellies are horrid, don't you? Beach parties are different. Can you ask your mother if you can come? Please do. It'll be lots of fun." She stood up, letting Peter run off along the prom.

"Well, we can't actually ask Mummy," Holly said, "but it'll be all right because we're very near the beach hut." Beth looked worried, but before she had a chance to say anything, Holly had an idea. "I know! We'll scratch a message to Mummy here on the prom, with a big arrow pointing to where we are. She'll easily see it, and she'd look on the beach anyway. We'd better not be long, though."

Marjorie's mother looked a little disapproving. Scratching on the prom was not what a well brought up young girl would do, but she smiled and said, "Well, then. We'll see you on the beach." She turned to talk to an elderly lady and they walked a little way down the prom together.

Holly found a pebble and was just scratching the first words when another little girl appeared beside Marjorie. She had fair hair and was dressed almost identically to her.

"*Bonjour. Je m'appelle Dulcie. J'ai une petite chat. J'ai une maison en Londres. Ou demeurez vous?*" (My name's Dulcie. I have a little cat. I have a house in London. Where do you live?)

Holly smiled and turned to Marjorie. "Is your cousin really French?" she asked. "She doesn't exactly sound French." Dulcie tried to look serious but didn't.

Marjorie laughed. "Oh no! She's English like me. But we've just started doing proper French sentences and we like to practise. Sometimes we practise on the way back from school. Grown-ups look very surprised. 'Oh, aren't those two little girls clever' they say. It's so funny! You see, until this term, we just learned some French words about farms but no proper sentences. There's a big picture of a farm on our classroom wall. We've learned '*mouton*' and '*vache*' and '*cochon*' and…"

"Cochon's rude," said Dulcie, laughing just like her cousin. "I know '*cheval*' and '*poulet*' and…"

"*Canard,*" added Marjorie.

"Yes, and, and, and… Oh, Godfrey Daniel's Blasted Iron Works!" shouted Dulcie, almost collapsing with mirth on the prom.

Beth, suddenly feeling quite at ease, burst out laughing, too. "What does THAT mean? Godfrey Daniel's what-his-name?"

Marjorie said, "Oh, that's Dulcie's special expression. She got it from Wilfred. That's her brother; he's thirteen. She only said it because she can't remember any more French words. I can. There's—"

"SOURIS!" shrieked Dulcie. "That's—"

"MOUSE!" shouted Marjorie, followed by more giggles.

Peter began to run ahead of them and then disappeared down some steps leading on to the beach. "Come on!" said Marjorie as she ran after him. "Come and meet Josh. You do really know him though, don't you?" she called out as she ran. "You must do because you were in—" she stopped for a moment to catch her breath. "You were in his beach hut. You're just pretending, aren't you? I like pretend games."

"But it's our beach hut," said Beth. "Our things were in it and—"

"I know. We'll pretend it is, shall we? Do you know," Marjorie said as she jumped down the steps one by one onto the shingle, "I always make friends on holiday. You see, I haven't got any brothers or sisters.

I wish I had, but I've got Dulcie and her house is just round the corner from mine. So she's my pretend sister."

They were all having such fun together, but as they followed Marjorie and Dulcie onto the beach, Holly was becoming more and more puzzled. *Who are they?* she thought, *and what has happened to us?* She looked at Beth, who now seemed quite unworried by the strangeness of it all and was chatting away to Marjorie and playing with Peter. Everything seemed so real, not a bit like a dream, and yet of course, nothing was real; it couldn't be. Could it?

The seafront had changed and yet not changed. Many of the buildings they could see from the prom looked familiar, but the King Alfred Leisure Centre had gone. The busy traffic had been replaced by one or two old-fashioned, open topped buses, the type the girls would sometimes see along the seafront in the summer months and at weekends. The sound of their engines mingled with the clip-clop of horses' hooves and the occasional "Whoa!" from the carriage drivers as they halted to let their passengers alight.

The prom under the children's bare feet felt warm and rough and hard. The sea, when they paddled in it later, felt cold and wet. Even Peter, as he shook the water from himself, felt warm and doggy. Yet Holly knew it could not be real. It was all something that must have happened a long time ago, but somehow they had entered into a dream together.

§ § § § §

Josh was about fourteen years old; he was quite tall with a big, slightly lop-sided grin and thick, black hair which flopped over his forehead and that he was continually pushing back. He wore a swimsuit similar in style to Marjorie's, except that it was sleeveless and the legs were longer. He, too, was friendly and introduced Holly and Beth to all the other children in their party. They soon felt as if they really did know him.

Josh began to explain the game of trenches to them. "What you do is," he said, picking up a big metal spade, "you dig a hole like this one. Of course, you can only play it here at low tide because of the stones."

He jumped down into the trench that was wide enough for three or four children to stand in side-by-side and deep enough for them to duck down. "You dig out a spadeful like this and then you pile the sand up round the trench like this," he said as he added his spadeful to the growing mound. "Another trench is dug a few yards away, as you can see. Then the boys in the trenches throw tennis balls at each other, and if you're hit, you're out. The girls are the ball boys. Oh, and if the tide starts coming in, run!"

He scrambled out and called the other children over. "Ah. I don't mean to be rude," he said to Holly, "but I see you're wearing boy's clothes. This could confuse the enemy."

Holly's cargo shorts and white T-shirt were startlingly out of place, but she had an odd feeling that if she explained that these were her normal clothes, the dream would shatter and the whole exciting adventure would be over. So she said nothing but picked up a straw hat one of the girls had left on a deckchair and put it on. "How about this? I can't look like a boy in this."

"Good tactics," Josh nodded approval. "So let battle commence!"

§ § § § §

Holly and Beth had not meant to be long on the beach, but now they noticed the sun seemed to be much lower and the tide was beginning to come in. Small waves broke on the shining pebbles with the iridescent glow of early evening and the children were chasing their long shadows across the shingle. It had been a happy afternoon and the time had flown by.

But then something rather extraordinary happened. They were both sitting playing five stones with Josh and Dulcie when Marjorie, who had run along the beach to talk to an older girl, came hurrying back.

"I've just heard Vera say something very important," she told them. "She's big, so she knows grown-up things. She said," and Marjorie pronounced it very clearly and slowly, "'Austria has declared war on Serbia.' Mother sounded worried. She said she thinks it will spread to our country soon. I didn't think we had wars anymore; I thought they only happened in history."

"Oh, but that happened in the First World War. We've just been learning a bit about it in history at school. It's—" Holly stopped suddenly, seeing the confused look on Marjorie's face.

"You are funny," she said. "You do say funny things! What's the First World War? There haven't been any wars that are in the *whole world*. Anyway, you can't learn about it in history; history's about things that happened a long time ago. We've been doing Romans. Have you done Romans? We've been learning about how they built long, straight roads. We've done lots of pictures of Romans." Marjorie's look of concern had gone and her mood had lightened.

"We did Romans last year," said Beth. "We made a fort, and Mrs. Tilley—she's my teacher—brought toy Roman soldiers for us to put in it. Don't take any notice of Holly; she's just showing off."

"We've got to go home now," said Holly, grabbing Beth's hand. "Thank you for a lovely afternoon. It was great playing trenches with Josh and everyone. Come to the beach hut again. Just knock on the door if it's shut. It's been really cool to meet your family, hasn't it, Beth?"

"What's cool? You do say funny things!" laughed Marjorie.

As the girls reached the beach hut, they turned to wave goodbye. Marjorie and Dulcie were balancing on the sea wall, waving back. Their small figures looked slightly hazy. Perhaps it was the effect of the warmth rising from the stone wall.

Holly and Beth had been back inside the beach hut for no more than a couple of minutes when they heard footsteps outside.

"Are you in there, girls?" called their mother. "I've got the tea here."

2

"My goodness, you look as if you've seen a ghost!"

Katy, the girls' mother, laughed when she saw the expression on their faces as she set the tea tray down on the little table. "I was quite quick today, wasn't I? Luckily, there were only a few people ahead of me in the queue. I've bought some buns, too. I expect you're starving after your swim."

Beth sat down on the bench and slowly picked up a bun, turning it over in her hand as if it were a strange object, but Holly, without saying a word, went outside. She seemed distracted and looked pale.

"Whatever is the matter with you two? Have you been arguing again?" asked Katy. "Did something happen in the few minutes I left you alone? You'd better tell me quickly if it did." She sounded rather anxious.

Holly came back inside, rubbing her eyes and blinking at the bright sunlight now pouring into the beach hut through its open doors. "I think I must have been dreaming. I don't understand. You said you were only a few minutes, but we've been hours on the beach. At least I thought we had. Beth, you were with me. Tell Mummy about what we did. And about the West Pier! Go on, you said you were dying to tell Mummy about it."

Beth picked up her mug of tea and said nothing.

"Beth, please! I'm sure I wasn't dreaming. Although, well, I suppose it can't really have happened. But it did happen, I know it did! You *were* there, Beth. You were scared in case Mummy couldn't find us. I scratched the message on the prom for Mummy. Maybe it's still there. Come on, let's go and look."

"I don't know what you're talking about. You must have been dreaming. I've just been here waiting for Mummy." Beth looked sullen and gave Holly a stubborn stare.

Katy sat down on the bench next to her. "Come and have your tea, Holly, and then we'll go along the prom and you can show me where you thought you scratched the message. Is that okay? But really, I was gone only a few minutes, maybe quarter of an hour at the most. There was barely time for you to have got dried and dressed and walked along the prom to write a message. Besides, I would have seen you. Don't you think you just might have dozed off? There were quite big waves, and it's always tiring swimming against them."

"Mummy, I know I didn't! How could I? There's not enough room in here to lie down, and the bench is too hard for me to have snoozed off sitting up. I just don't understand. We had a brilliant afternoon. Beth knows!"

"Shut up, Holly. You're stupid. You were dreaming; I saw you asleep. You—"

"That's a lie, Beth! How can you say such things? Mummy, she joined in all the games and everything. She—"

"I did not! I won't talk about it 'cos I wasn't there. I want to have my tea. Shut up!"

Beth picked up her mug but stared at Holly over the top of it

"All right," said Katy, "I've had enough of this. I'm taking the tea outside, and we're going to be quiet and civilised while we have it. Then Holly can tell me all about her dream—without interruptions from you, Beth." Katy picked up the tea tray and set it down on the step, then went back in to collect some deck chairs. "And Beth, you'd better take off that wet swimsuit and get dressed. The wind's getting up, and that damp towel won't keep you warm. I should put on your fleece. We'd better hurry up with our tea."

Although the sun was still bright, a freshening wind was catching at a polythene bag and chocolate wrappers someone had carelessly discarded on the prom and was bowling them along, lifting them up into the air. A young man on roller blades flew past, the wind filling his nylon jacket, billowing it out like a yellow sail and whipping the surface of the sea into white horses. Somewhere farther down the row of beach huts, a door banged relentlessly.

Holly, who had just sat down in a deck chair, sprang up, almost knocking over the tea tray.

"That's it!" she shouted, grabbing Beth's towel from her. "It's not damp at all, and her swimsuit's completely dry. That proves it; you can't lie about it now, Beth. You were with us on the beach all afternoon."

Beth seized the towel from her sister and ran into the beach hut, slamming the door which sprang open again in the wind. "It got dry just now in the sun, stupid! Or the wind. Leave me alone."

"I don't think we can talk about this any longer," said Katy, quickly gathering up the tray and half eaten buns. "Look at that black cloud— it's going to get us any minute. Quick, help me get everything back inside, Holly, there's a dear. We're going to have to run for the car."

Big raindrops were marking the prom with an ever-growing pattern of dark spots. People were hurrying off the beach, towels held over their heads, some struggling to pull on cagoules. In a matter of moments, the sea had turned from greenish blue to a leaden grey. The town was almost obscured by a sheet of rain. The skeleton of the West Pier stood forlornly, its broken windows dark and empty, the tattered remains of curtains flapping in the wind and wrapping themselves around the paintless window frame. As far as the eye could see, there was no break in the expanse of greyness that merged sea and sky on the invisible horizon. The sudden change was quite startling.

In the car on the way home, none of them spoke very much. Katy, although having to concentrate on driving in torrential rain and the heavy traffic that had appeared from nowhere, was lost in her own thoughts. How could Beth's swimsuit and towel be dry? It certainly was very odd. And Holly was so sure she hadn't been dreaming. But none of it made sense; it was a complete mystery. She'd have to have a talk with Holly on her own. She hoped both girls would be in a better mood by the time they got home. Katy could see in the rearview mirror that Beth was giving Holly one of her defiant looks; Holly had gone strangely quiet, staring out of the window and hugging her duffel bag on her lap.

Well, maybe some hot buttered toast and more tea would cheer them all up.

The rain looked set to continue for the whole evening. The girls had gone upstairs, and Katy could hear them arguing while she put on the kettle and laid the table. Well, there was nothing she could do until after they'd all eaten and then, hopefully, Holly and Beth would be in better moods.

She had just called them down when the doorbell rang. "You start," she said, "I won't be a minute. It's probably Mrs. Dawson from next-door come to collect her key. She's due back from holiday this evening."

The girls could hear their mother talking at the front door. "Yes, it's fine, really. Of course she can stay. I hope you enjoy the play, and don't worry at all. Honestly, it's no problem."

"Doesn't sound like Mrs. Dawson," said Holly, who had been buttering her toast in silence. "It would be funny if *she* came to stay."

Beth giggled. In the cosiness of a wet summer teatime, everything seemed to be returning to normal.

Katy came into the kitchen carrying a small holdall and accompanied by a little girl who was clutching a Barbie doll in one hand and a rather battered teddy bear in the other.

"Alice has come to stay for the night. Her parents are going to the theatre and she was supposed to be staying at her granny's, but her poor granny has had a fall and is not very well. Perhaps Alice could have the bottom bunk in your room, Beth?"

Alice Bowman was at the same school as Beth, but she was a year younger. She lived in the same road and the girls often played together.

"Cool!" said Beth. "Can we go and watch 'Top of the Pops' after tea, Mum? Look at Alice's new Barbie—she's really nice. She's got sparkly bits in her hair."

They were soon all chatting away over their tea and toast, making important decisions as to who would have the last remains of the chocolate spread and who would open the new jar of peanut butter. It was an evening just like so many evenings; it had a comfortable, familiar feel about it, nothing out of the ordinary and nothing to mark it as unusual in any way. The long, sun-drenched afternoon playing happily on the beach with children who appeared to have come from another time seemed a million miles away, a different world. Holly glanced out of the window at the rain splashing into the fishpond and running in rivulets down the garden steps to the patio. Some of the washing had been left out on the line: there were her new jeans, her cycling shorts, and Beth's yellow Brownie sweatshirt hanging limply beside a double duvet cover. Beth's new scooter stood propped against the garden shed, their father's racing bike next to it, just as it had been the day before.

Holly glanced at the clock on the mantelpiece. The hands showed it was a quarter to seven. She looked at her watch; the time was the same. Everything seemed to be normal, and yet that afternoon in the beach hut, time had almost stood still and somehow moved years backwards simultaneously. So could it all have been a dream? No, oh no; it was just not possible.

After tea, Beth ran upstairs to get her own collection of Barbie dolls, and she and Alice went into the lounge together to watch 'Top of the Pops.' Holly stayed sitting at the tea table with her mother.

"Mummy, I know it sounds really silly, and I know you'll never believe me that it really did happen. I can hardly believe it myself now we're home and it's pouring with rain and everything's normal. But can I just tell you about it? Beth and Alice are far too busy to come and interrupt us."

"Go on," said Katy, "I'm listening."

"Okay. Well. This is what happened. You'd hardly gone more than a few minutes when there was a knock at the door. It was a little girl who said her name was Mar... Margaret."

Something inexplicable made Holly want to keep Marjorie's real name to herself. It was almost as if to tell the whole story would spoil the magic of it. It didn't seem like telling a lie because maybe none of it really happened anyway. But Holly described to her mother all that she and Beth and their newfound friends had done together. She described the West Pier, alive with people and colour and movement. She explained the games they'd all played together and the clothes the children and the grown-ups had been wearing. Holly nearly told her mother about the extraordinary thing that Marjorie had heard from her friend Vera at the end of the afternoon, but that seemed just too unbelievable. She decided she'd say nothing about that, at least for the time being.

"And, Mummy, I just know that Beth really was there with me, whatever she says now. And I know how I can get her to admit it. I'm going to trick her into giving herself away, and then if she does, you'll know it can't have been a dream. You do believe me, don't you? I mean you don't really think I could have made all this up? Do you?"

Katy looked thoughtful. Holly's descriptions were very vivid and, thinking of books she'd read about old Brighton, extraordinarily accurate.

"Well, you could have seen pictures in the museum which caught your imagination so much that you dreamed about them. From what you've been telling me, I should think the time you dreamed about—"

"Mummy!"

"Okay, or somehow experienced, must have been around the early part of the last century. We could go and have a look at the museum tomorrow. If it's still raining hard, it would be a good thing to do. Would you like to do that? Daddy might like to come, too."

"You know Daddy will never believe me. He'll just think I'm playing a game or something. Anyway, I thought he wanted to go the football match."

"Oh yes, I'd forgotten. And he wanted you to go with him," said Katy.

"Yes, but I don't really want to if it's pouring with rain. I'm sure he won't mind."

And so it was decided. The following afternoon, which was Saturday, Katy and the girls would go to the museum and do some research. Holly felt a lot happier now that her mother was taking her seriously, but she was still unsure she believed her.

"Can I phone Granny?" she asked. "I want to tell her about everything. I'm sure she'd understand, and she likes me to phone, I know she does." Her grandmother would never laugh at her and—this was important—she almost always got the history questions right in general knowledge quizzes.

"Oh, I'm so sorry, darling. She and Grandpa left for Canada this morning. Do you remember, I told you they were going out to help Aunty Rachel?" Katy was genuinely sorry. She would have liked to talk to her mother herself about Holly's extraordinary story. "You know Aunty Rachel's baby is due any day now? Granny and Grandpa put off going for as long as possible because Great-Granny's been so poorly since her stroke, but they wanted to be there to look after little Luke when the baby's born." Rachel was Katy's younger sister; the girls' cousin, three-year-old Luke, was quite a handful. "I don't think this is something you could really explain in a short transatlantic phone call. Wait till Granny and Grandpa have come home. They're due back at the end of August if all goes well."

§ § § § § §

Alice's parents called early the next morning to pick her up. She was yawning hard and looking very sleepy when she appeared on the stairs with her holdall, Teddy's paw sticking out of the zip at one end. Beth sat on the top stair, still in her pyjamas.

Mrs. Bowman laughed. "I see you two have had a good night's sleep! What was it then—a midnight feast, or too much telly?"

"It wasn't exactly at midnight. Anyway, Beth's mum didn't mind. She said it was all right as long as we didn't talk all night." Alice turned to Katy with an endearing smile.

"And were you talking all night?" asked Mr. Bowman as he gave Alice a hug.

"Not exactly *all* night. But Beth kept wanting to tell me stories. She called it her 'Mystery Adventure.' I wish I could make up stories like Beth. It was really exciting! It was all about—"

"NO! You mustn't tell anyone; it will spoil it!" Beth shouted down the stairs. "Don't tell ANYONE, or I won't make up any more next time you stay. You promised."

Katy picked up Alice's cagoule that was hanging on the banisters. "I think she'll be needing this; it looks as if it's still raining. You'd never think it was the end of July, would you? And don't worry about the stories. Beth has a great sense of imagination. I think they've both had a lot of fun, certainly judging by the giggles we heard last night."

"Don't forget!" Beth called out as Alice and her parents were saying their "thank yous" and were about to leave. "You promised."

3

The museum is a place of wonderment. Upon entering, the visitor is greeted by an enormous papier-mâché cat whose glass-windowed tummy reveals a large collection of coins. And if that visitor should decide to add to the cat's money meal, he or she will be surprised by a growly "Thank You" from deep inside the cat's interior.

Then there is the Cabinet of Curios, with its drawers full of the strangest things: fossils hidden from sight for thousands of years; a shell, whose mother-of-pearl interior is lined with velvet and cradles a little ivory doll; a tiny kaleidoscope that, when held to the eye, reveals a scene from the 1851 Great Exhibition; all manner of curious things.

Upstairs, there are sedan chairs and Victorian bicycles and—a special favourite of all the children—a little donkey cart which used to ply the seafront and a real, stuffed donkey in the harness. There are costumes from many a bygone age, old photographs revealing their own stories of times long gone, and stuffed birds and butterflies, and whole rooms set out just as they would have looked fifty or a hundred or several hundreds of years ago.

One such room immediately caught Holly's attention. The familiarity of it startled her; not the room so much as the clothes the waxwork models were wearing. There, worn by a little girl with long, fair hair tied up with a large black bow, was the dress—or one remarkably like it—that had been hanging up in the beach hut the day before: Marjorie's dress!

This was when an idea struck Holly that might, just possibly, trick Beth into telling the truth.

"Look, Beth!" said Holly. "Look at this dress—it's just like the red one we saw hanging up in the beach hut."

"It wasn't red, stupid, it was..." Beth had fallen right into the trap.

"Mummy! Did you hear what Beth said? That proves that she was there. She saw the dress, and she knows it was dark blue. Go on, Beth, you've got to tell Mummy now. You can't go on pretending it never happened. Go on, tell her!"

"Tell her what? I want to go and look at the butterflies."

In a second, Beth was out of the room and running along the polished wooden floor, her footsteps echoing on the hollow boards. Past waxwork gentlemen with full-bottomed wigs and embroidered top-coats, past stately ladies in regency ball gowns of blue and lavender silk, past a nursemaid holding the curved wooden handle of a beautiful coach built pram, and finally she was on to the stairs.

"Whoa! Not so fast, young lady."

It was the curator of the museum himself who caught Beth as she was about to tumble.

"Why in such a hurry to leave? I don't know what our nursemaid there would think of a little girl running off in such an unladylike way. Did she frighten you? She's very kindly really; my staff call her Aggie."

The curator, whose name was Mr. Edwards, had just set Beth down safely at the top of the flight of stairs when Katy and Holly arrived.

"I'm *so* sorry," said Katy. "I don't know what came over my daughter. Beth, you could have fallen all the way down those stairs; thank goodness Mr. Edwards was here to catch you. I'm so sorry," she repeated to the curator. "I'll make quite sure she stays with us now."

"Oh, don't you worry about it at all," said Mr. Edwards, who was a kindly man. "All we wish for at the museum is that our visitors enjoy themselves and learn some of our fascinating history along the way. So, what was it you were in such a hurry to see, young lady?"

"I wanted to see the butterflies, but Holly was trying to stop me." Beth glared at her sister.

"Well now, they're not going to fly away, you know. In fact, some of them, especially the rare ones, have been in their cases for a very long time. Would you like me to show you my favourites? Perhaps your mother and sister would like to come, too."

Holly's frustration at having failed to persuade Beth to admit to anything concerning their adventure of the day before was almost too much to bear. If only she had been able to stop her from running off! But she dutifully accompanied her mother and Beth down the wide stone staircase to the Natural History gallery.

"Here we are," said Mr. Edwards as he began to pull out case after case of the most beautiful butterflies, from the tiniest blues to some from the forests of New Guinea that were a vivid gold, green, blue and black and were as wide across as a man's hand. "Did you know there are about twelve thousand different species of butterfly? Now, let's just try this cabinet here to see if I can find Samson."

Mr. Edwards opened yet another cabinet in the far corner of the room. "Yes, here he is. He's not very rare as he's a swallowtail from our own Great Britain. But look at his wonderful colours and exquisite markings. Don't you just love him?"

'Samson' was indeed a beautiful specimen, and it wasn't too hard for Beth to appear to be completely engrossed in the collection of which Mr. Edwards was so proud. But Holly was desperate to get away and to return to the costume gallery. She did not want to seem rude, so it was necessary for her to think quickly of a good reason to leave the butterfly room.

"Oh no!" said Holly as Mr. Edwards was removing the case containing Samson in order that Beth might have a closer look. "I'm really sorry, but I must have dropped my pen upstairs. It was with my notebook. It was the one Granny gave me, and I don't want to lose it. I'll just go back to where we were before; it's probably fallen on the floor."

As Holly reached the door of the butterfly room, she turned to her mother. "Don't worry if I'm a few minutes. I just want to make some notes for a project we might be doing next term. I'll come back here to find you."

"Very commendable," said Mr. Edwards as Holly hurried from the Natural History gallery. "Just what I like to hear—a young person who is interested enough to take notes. She should go far. Now," he turned to Beth, "let me get a magnifying glass for you to take a closer look at Samson."

Holly breathed a sigh of relief as she rounded the corner to the staircase and, when she was sure that she was out of sight, was soon taking the steps two at a time.

Standing once more in front of the room setting, which had seemed so strangely familiar, Holly was able to take in more detail. It really was an extraordinary thing: the waxwork models of the little girl and the lady standing next to her, although their faces were nothing like that of Marjorie or her mother, looked almost like old friends. *It was quite ridiculous,* she thought, but if there had been models wearing T-shirts and jeans, they would have seemed no more familiar than the two now in front of her. Their clothes might be a bit different from hers, but they were still just normal, everyday clothes.

Holly found herself laughing out loud; it was quite absurd! Then she suddenly remembered she hadn't much time; if she spent too long up here, her mother would surely come looking for her. She would need to concentrate.

A notice told her the room was a parlour. On the wall above a small cast-iron fireplace hung a tinted portrait photograph of King Edward VII and Queen Alexandra in a rather ornate frame. Over the door to the right of the fireplace was an oblong glass case about eighteen inches long containing a number of flat metal springs, similar to those in a clockwork mechanism but larger, with a bell attached to each one. Against the opposite wall stood an upright piano with brass sconces to hold candles, and a panel of red pleated silk in the middle of the wooden frame of the piano behind the rest where an open book of music was balanced. On a small, round table next to the piano stood a potted palm.

Holly was determined to remember as much detail as possible of the room. She wanted to be able to imagine the sort of house in which Marjorie would have lived. She took notes, every now and then glancing at the room and the two waxwork models. After a few minutes, the little girl and her mother were beginning to look almost real. Holly found herself smiling at them and—no, surely not—could the little girl have winked at her just now? That was just too ridiculous!

"The piano's Victorian, so not quite contemporary with the room," said a voice behind her.

Holly jumped, dropping her notebook and pen.

"My goodness, if it isn't our nursemaid Aggie causing alarm, it's me," said Mr. Edwards. "Well, now. How are you getting on? Your sister's much taken with Samson; she's drawing a picture of him."

"Oh, uh, fine, thank you." Holly hurriedly stuffed her notebook into her jeans pocket.

"As I was saying," continued Mr. Edwards, "the piano is older than the other exhibits in the room. Do you see the candle sconces? By this time, say about 1913 or 1914, most houses, like the one in which this room might have been, would have had gaslight, perhaps even electricity. But before the days of radio and television, people made their own entertainment and a family singsong round the piano was the equivalent of a family of today watching the television together, but much friendlier. Do you see the title of the sheet music?"

Holly had already noted that. She wondered if Marjorie knew it; perhaps she'd ask her when they next met. She didn't doubt for a minute they would meet again.

"Yes, it's 'Two Lovely Black Eyes.' Do you know how it goes?"

"I most certainly do; it was my granddad's favourite. We mustn't make too much noise because other visitors might complain, and we couldn't have that, could we? But there's no one here just now, so I'll just give you a little snatch of the tune."

Mr. Edwards cleared his throat. Swaying slightly and with elbows bent, he broke into song. His deep, bass voice boomed out cheerfully just as Katy and Beth arrived back in the gallery. Oblivious of the small crowd that had gathered, he finished the song to riotous applause.

"Oh dear, oh dear," he said, with a beaming smile. "I seem to have shattered the peace and quiet somewhat; Aggie will be telling me off next. However," he said with a small bow to his audience, "thank you for your kind appreciation. Just adding a little touch of the period for our young visitors here. You see," he said, turning to the girls, "this was a very popular Music Hall song and sheet music for songs like this would have been sold in large numbers, much like a recording of a song that's in the charts today."

The crowd began to disperse, looking the happier for their impromptu entertainment.

Mr. Edwards was highly regarded, and it was not unusual for him to add something special to make a visit to the museum memorable.

"Did you say Music Hall?" Holly remembered Marjorie had said something about a music hall; whatever was it? Oh yes, that was it! Her cousin Morris was called Josh because Auntie Hettie had heard a song about a boy called Josh at the Music Hall. "What is a music hall?" she asked. "I heard someone mention one the other day."

Beth looked uncomfortable but clutched her brightly coloured picture of Samson and said nothing.

"The Music Hall," said Mr. Edwards, "was very popular in the early part of the last century. It was rather like a concert, but there were comedy acts, too. Some of the songs were rather naughty! Many of the singers and comedians became very well known, like pop stars of today. The entertainment started in the nineteenth century in concert halls attached to public houses, but soon grew to take over theatres under licence. In their heyday, it was reckoned that in London alone about twenty-five million people a year would visit music halls."

Beth, who had suddenly started to take an interest, was looking intently at the room setting.

"What are those things in there?" she asked Mr. Edwards, pointing to the glass case above the door in the parlour.

"Ah, now. We've been told off for having those bells in the parlour. A very old lady pointed out, quite correctly, that they should be in the kitchen. When a bell rang, the maid would look at the name under it—can you see the names?—and she would know in which room she was required. Say it was the drawing room. She'd quickly straighten her cap and apron, which would be white over a black dress for afternoon or evening when visitors might be expected, and she'd hurry along to ask what was needed. You see, there would be a bell pull in every room which connected with that contrivance you're looking at."

A very old lady? If Marjorie were still alive, thought Holly, *she'd be a very old lady by now.* She quickly pushed the thought from her mind. Marjorie was little girl on a bright, sunny beach. After all, hadn't they seen her only yesterday?

"So why is it in the parlour?" asked Beth, whose interest seemed to be growing.

"There's little story attached to that," said Mr. Edwards. "As you know, our museum isn't very large, and we don't have enough space here for another room setting from this period. The items displayed in this room are, in fact, a little mixed as regards their age but then so they would have been at the time. The photograph on the wall is of King Edward VII and Queen Alexandra and much of the furniture is Edwardian. But the clothes would have been worn a few years after the king's death, in the reign of George V. Now, the bells. We particularly wanted to display the bells because they were a gift from another old lady, Mrs. Hawkes-Lewis. She used to live in one of the big old houses in St. Aubyn's. Her house was the very last one to be converted into flats; most of them have been flats for many years."

"I know St. Aubyn's," said Holly, "It's near the King Alfred Leisure Centre."

"Quite right, young lady. So you'll know just the kind of house I'm talking about," said Mr. Edwards, "very tall, some five storeys high and quite narrow. When Mrs. Hawkes-Lewis left her house to move into a bungalow in Rottingdean—she was having great difficulty with all those stairs, and the house was much too big for her—her family sold most of the contents of the house at auction. But she asked to be taken back for one last look before the builders moved in. The house was quite empty, but there in the kitchen the bells were still securely on the wall in their glass case."

"So she took them down and gave them to you?" asked Beth.

"They were screwed very firmly to the wall, but she asked her son to take them down. When she gave them to us, she said they brought back some happy memories and that one day she'd tell me all about it. I hope she does; so many wonderful stories are lost because they are not recorded."

Mr.Edwards looked thoughtful, as if he himself were recollecting. He turned to both the girls, serious, but still with a smile.

"You make sure, now, that your granny, or great-granny or great-great aunt or uncle writes down all they can remember about their childhood while they can still write. Take a tape recorder along to them otherwise. We must never forget that everything that happened in the past is part of the present and the future. Now," he said, his sombre mood gone, "I have to go and have my lunch, and I expect you will, too. But before I go, perhaps you'd all like to come down to reception with me. I've got something for Holly—it is Holly, isn't it?—that she might find useful."

They followed Mr. Edwards down the stone staircase to the ground floor. From a cupboard behind the reception desk, he took out a folder and gave it to Holly. It was made of mottled orange card with a pattern rather like the bookplates at the front of a very old encyclopaedia. On the cover was a picture of the museum cat. Inside there were several pages describing the museum and how to find what you're looking for and lots of useful information about the exhibits. There was a pocket for postcards, a clip for a pen, and about a dozen or so blank pages for making notes and drawings. The folder had black elastic on the corners, securing everything firmly in place.

"Now you won't need to lose your pen." Mr. Edwards winked at Holly; could he have guessed her deception? "Or your notes. Come and tell me about your project when you've finished."

Holly liked it. The cat's broad grin and the expression in its painted eyes made it look as if it had a secret to hide, a secret to be revealed only to the owner of the folder.

"Thank you very much," she said, as she put it carefully into the bag with the shopping that Miss Jones, guessing that it might be forgotten, had collected for them from the cloakroom. "It will be really useful. It'll help me to find out about stuff for my project. There's so much more I want to see. I'll be able to do my notes and drawings in it. I love the cat on the front. It's really kind of you "

Mr. Edwards picked up his umbrella and was saying goodbye to Katy and the girls and that he hoped he'd see them all again soon when Holly remembered something.

"Oh, Mr. Edwards," she said, "Do you know what Mrs. Hawkes-Lewis's Christian name is?"

"I do believe I do. Let me think, now. Yes, it's Amelia. Amelia Elspeth."

4

It rained for nearly two weeks. On the promenade stretching west along the seafront from the Palace Pier, only the bravest and hardiest visitors joined the regulars, some with their hoods pulled down against the driving rain and others almost revelling in it, laughing and splashing in the puddles with a solid determination not to let anything ruin their holiday.

To add to the misery of the less active but die-hard visitors huddled in the seaside shelters, a strong wind had blown in from the southwest. It churned the grey sea into a boiling mass of breakers that hurled small stones across the prom right up to the summer-sandalled feet of the shelterers. It set the café signs swinging, overturned rubbish bins, and caught at the plastic windbreaks of the seaside tea bars, wrenching some from their moorings.

The old West Pier was a more sorrowful sight than ever. Huge breakers battered the iron girders of its fragile structure. The few black empty windows, which still remained intact, looked in danger of shattering under the force of the wind and the hail of stones sucked up from the beach in the enormous waves. Even the seagulls with their eerie, mournful cries seemed to sense the gloom of the morning.

"Honestly, Holly, I can't think why you want to go to the beach hut now," said Katy as she battled with her umbrella, which had turned inside out for the fourth time and was in danger of collapsing. "This is crazy! I'm going to have to put this brolly down, or it will definitely break. It's no good dashing ahead because I've got the key. Why is it so important that we go now?"

"Because we might be able to..." Holly's answer was lost in the wind.

Beth had gone to her Art and Crafts Holiday club at school and would not be back until lunchtime. They had dropped her off and had come straight down to the seafront, much against Katy's better judgment, but Holly was so insistent that she had given in.

Thank goodness, thought Katy, *for the school holiday clubs;* they ran for only a week, but on a day like this, they were a real blessing. Holly had Science Workshop that afternoon, and Beth would be playing at a friend's house until teatime. But if this weather continued, she decided, they'd just have to book a holiday somewhere abroad, even if it was at the last minute. She'd talk about it to Stephen tonight. She knew what he'd say, that he could not possibly take time off from the business at the moment, but somehow she'd have to persuade him.

Lost in her thoughts, Katy realised they had arrived at the beach hut.

"Come on, Mummy! Have you got the key? Let's get in out of the rain." Holly's hood had blown off; her wet hair was clinging to her face and water was dripping coldly down her neck. "It'll be okay in a minute; I know it will."

Katy fumbled for the key, her hands numb from the cold rain. Just as she was about to unlock the padlock, a stooping figure in a very wet parka and an old fisherman's hat came hurrying towards them. It was Jim, who kept a watchful eye on all the beach huts along the promenade.

"Oh, Mrs. Randall, ma'am."

Katy always wondered why Jim addressed her in this royal way, but secretly rather liked it. "I'm awful pleased to see you, ma'am. I was gonna phone you, but now I've seen you, that's better still." Jim pulled out a large red handkerchief to dry his glasses. After carefully replacing them, with a few minor adjustments, he continued. "Last Tuesday I was down 'ere, ma'am, checking up on all my little 'ouses as usual, when I noticed—"

"Why don't you come inside a minute, Jim, to be out of the rain?" interrupted Katy, who by now had managed to open the padlock and let Holly in. "You can tell me what the problem is. I might even be able to make us a cup of tea if there's enough gas."

"Thank you, ma'am, I will step inside if that's all right. But I won't stop for tea 'cos I 'ave me duties to attend to. This 'ere wind's causing 'avoc with the newer 'uts." He took off his hat and sat down on one of the yellow benches. "This 'ut's a good'n, built strong and firm she is;

but you take number seventy-three, now. Smashed to smithereens, she
is, in that there storm last night. Mrs. Clarke'd left her dinghy blown
up and it were out across the prom, battered against the wall. She'll
not be taking the kiddies out in that again."

"You were saying, about our beach hut," Katy gently urged Jim to
get back to the point.

"Oh yes, ma'am. Well, as I was saying, I came down last Tuesday
on me usual duties, and I noticed your doors were just a bit ajar and
the padlock were undone. I thought to meself, that's odd, Mrs. Randall always locks up proper. So I goes to shut the door and do up the
padlock. But first I thinks to meself, better check that no burglar come
in, like, and nicked anything. Not that I'd know what you 'ad in 'ere,
ma'am, but I've a good eye for things what's amiss."

Jim paused and glanced at Katy and Holly, whose curiosity she
could hardly contain, to check what impact his story was having. Sat-
isfied he had their full attention, he continued.

"Now, at a quick glance, ma'am, nothing seemed to be missing.
The gas 'ob were there, yer tins 'o tea, yer mugs, yer deck chairs.
Stuff that most of me ladies and gents keep in their 'uts. But 'ere's the
strange thing, ma'am. There was sand on the floor, and little kiddies'
footprints." Jim paused again, shifting slightly on the bench. Holly
caught her breath, her heart beating fast. She looked down at the floor,
but there was nothing to see but the slightly muddy bare boards and
the damp coir mat.

"Oh, you won't see nothing now, Miss Holly; this 'ere sou'west-
erly blows under the doors and through the cracks. What wi' that and
a bit o' rain in the wind and you won't see nothing left. But I'm telling you, they was there."

"Perhaps someone broke in?" Katy suggested. "The padlock's
probably quite easy to force. At least there's been no harm done and
you're right, nothing seems to have been stolen."

"No, but what you don't see, ma'am, is this. That there padlock
ain't been forced, and even if someone 'ad come in all right and
proper, 'ow could there be *sand* on the floor? You only get sand at the
spring tides, don't yer, ma'am; and what 'ave we had these past couple o' weeks? Neap tides. No sand. Tide don't go out that far. Nearest
kiddies' sandpit? Three 'undred yards down the prom. And it's full o'
water wi' all this rain. And another thing, ma'am. I found a little kiddie's belt on the floor, made of some kind of elastic wi' a sort of little
buckle on it. Unusual, it were. I 'ung it up just there, above Miss
Holly's 'ead."

Holly leaped up to look above her head. There was nothing there. She stood on the bench to look on the shelf where they kept the tea and biscuits; she knelt down on the wooden floor and looked under the bench. Nothing.

"Are you sure it was this side, Mr. Jim?" Holly always addressed him as Mr. Jim in deference to his 'Miss Holly' It seemed the polite thing to do. "Are you really, really sure? Mummy, you look your side. We've got to find it. We've just got to."

Holly was pushing the tins and mugs along the shelf above the hob, pulling down tea towels and packets of biscuits in her urgency to find some evidence of Marjorie's having visited. She was so sure she was on the edge of discovering something important.

"It weren't anything valuable, Miss Holly. Just a kiddie's belt. Funny it ain't where I put it, though. Don't get yourself worked up about it, now. But I'm just thinking to meself, could they 'ave been back since last Tuesday? I dunno. I can't make it out. We've 'ad solid rain for nearly two weeks, ain't we, ma'am? I thought about it, and I thought about it, but I can't work out where that sand come from. And the footmarks made with a little kiddie's bare feet. Not the weather for it. Not the weather for it at all."

"What size were the footmarks?" asked Holly, anxious for more clues. "I mean, were they really small, like a little toddler's?"

"No, Miss Holly, not that small. At a guess, going by me own grandchildren, about the size of Miss Beth's, give or take a size either way. Come to think of it, there could have been two kiddies. There was certainly quite a lot o' little footmarks, as if they'd been jumping up and down or dancing around. Anyway, no 'arm done." Jim got up, pulling his parka round him and putting on his hat. "But maybe, ma'am," he turned to Katy, "you might give a thought to a new padlock. I'm thinking maybe someone 'as your key. You didn't lend it to no one, did you, and forget about it?"

"No, absolutely not," Katy assured him. "We often have friends down here, but only when we're here ourselves. In fact, I've only got one key. I keep meaning to get another cut in case this one gets lost, but I've never got round to it. I'll take your advice and get a new padlock."

"No!" Holly grabbed her mother's arm. "You mustn't do that. I mean, er…"

"Well, I'll leave it with you, ma'am. I'd best be on me way now. I gotta telephone Mrs. Clarke and tell 'er the bad news. Number twenty-one ain't in too good a shape, neither. Roof looks as if it could be off in the next storm. So goodbye to you now, and don't you worry, I'll be keeping an eye on things."

He tipped his old fisherman's hat to them and walked off down the prom, checking the doors of all the beach huts as he went.

Holly leaned out of the doors to watch him go, and then she turned back to her mother, pulling the doors closed behind her.

"You see, Mummy? You've just got to believe me now! It's obvious! Marj—" She just stopped herself, still determined to keep Marjorie's real name to herself. It didn't make any sense, but somehow it just seemed the right thing to do. "Margaret has been here! And in her time it isn't rain, rain, rain. It's proper summer weather, and there's sand to play in. Please, please let's see now if we can get back there." Holly flung her arms round her mother's neck. "We've just got to try."

"I think we should make a cup of tea first. I need a few minutes to think. It's too much to take in; I mean, the idea that somehow, by going out of this beach hut, we could go back to 1914 and a fine summer's day." Katy handed the empty kettle to Holly. "I'm beginning to think I'm dreaming now. Anyway, you go and fill up the kettle, and we'll talk about it."

Holly took the kettle and opened the door. Could it have already happened? Could they even now be transported back all those years? No, the rain was as heavy as ever, and there was the old West Pier as forlorn as ever.

"I don't want to talk about it—I want to go there! Oh, all right, I'll fill the kettle. I hope there are still some Jaffa Cakes left."

Ten minutes later, with mugs of hot tea to warm them and the few remaining Jaffa Cakes to eat, Katy said, "You know, Jim could have been mistaken. About the padlock, I mean. I don't know how he could have been so sure that it hadn't been forced. Some children could have come in and played here, out of the rain. Maybe they filled their buckets with sand before the sandpit was flooded. It is possible, you know."

"You just want there to be a sensible explanation, but there isn't one. Don't you want to believe it could happen? Honestly, Mummy, you'd love it. It was brilliant. It was as if we'd known them all for years when we said goodbye." Holly's excitement was mounting. "There are lots of things that happen that don't seem possible. What about email and the Internet and stuff? No one would have believed they were possible when you were a little girl. Let's just try, *please!*"

"How did it happen, then? You show me." Katy finished her tea and leaned back on the bench. *I must be mad,* she thought. How could she even for a second believe this nonsense? She'd laugh about it later.

"Okay. Now, Beth and I were just sitting here when Margaret"— Holly got it right that time—"knocked on the door and we let her in. We talked for a bit, as I told you, and then when we opened the doors, there we were in 1914. We didn't know then it was 1914, of course. Not until, well, not until later. Now, there's no one knocking on the door but perhaps if we really believe it will happen, it will. Do you want it to happen?"

"It would be good to get out of the rain for a while; the thought of a sunny beach at this moment is very appealing. Right, I'll try. I'm willing us to be able to go back in time." Katy shut her eyes.

"Me too. Okay. In a minute I'm going to open the doors," said Holly. "Ready?"

"Ready. No, wait a minute. We might be gone for hours; what about Beth?" Katy couldn't believe what she was saying. Was she really going along with this crazy idea?

"Mummy, I told you! Time stands still in 2001. Well, almost. Ready?"

"Okay. Ready."

Holly was trembling as she turned the handle of the door. It seemed that for a split second she saw sunlight, but when she opened the door, she could have cried. There was the rain-soaked prom and everything just as it had been when they arrived.

"Why? Why hasn't it worked? I don't understand! What have I done wrong?" She sank back onto the bench, very near to tears.

Katy put her arms round her. "What we should be asking is not why didn't it happen now, but why did it happen when it did? After all, we've had the beach hut for a few years now, and nothing like this has ever happened before."

"But it did happen. It did, it did! You're going to think I'm going mad or something. But it was lovely. It wasn't spooky or anything. Beth was scared for a minute because she thought we wouldn't be able to get back, but I never thought that for a second. Not really. Well, maybe a second, but not much more."

"Well, if there is a reason, it will happen again. And I am trying to believe you, I really am. But let's go home now and get on some dry clothes and start getting lunch ready. I don't want you to be late for Science Workshop. We'll leave washing the mugs up until next time. It's just too wet now even to go to the tap for the water."

"We could try one more time," said Holly. "We could wait a few minutes and then try."

"Well, shut the doors again. We'll have to open them to go out anyway, but I don't see that there's any point in waiting."

Holly shut the doors, took a deep breath, and slowly opened them again, just a crack at first as if by doing so she could slow down time and allow whatever made it happen to happen again. But it was no good. They stepped out into the rain, carefully closed the doors behind them, and fastened the padlock.

"You won't change the lock, will you, Mummy?"

"No, I'll leave it as it is for now," Katy said as she put the key in her bag. "We'd better run for the car." There was no one now on the prom except an elderly man in an old-fashioned yellow sou'wester leading a very bedraggled dog.

§ § § § §

Later that day, when Katy had finished all the ironing and housework while both the girls were out for the afternoon, the weather at last began to cheer up. She went into the front garden to do some weeding; it was such easy work when the ground was so wet. She looked up at the clouds to see a small patch of blue sky appearing. "Just big enough to mend a sailor's trousers," she said to herself, smiling as she remembered her granny's expression.

Just before five o'clock, Beth came running up the drive holding a beautiful bright orange papier-mâché plate decorated with little gold stars.

"Look, Mummy! This is what I made today. I made it for you. And Daddy. Do you like it?"

"Darling, it's lovely. You're a very clever girl. I shall put it up in the kitchen for Daddy to see when he gets home. Now that you're back, I'll go and get the tea. Oh, here's Holly, too. That's great, we'll all have tea together." Katy put her trowel and fork in the basket with the weeds and stood up, rubbing the mud from her hands.

"How was Science Workshop?" she called out to Holly as she opened the gate.

"It was brilliant, absolutely brilliant! I've got something really special to tell you. Can we have tea? I'm starving!"

Soon, the three of them were sitting down together with tea and toast and some fruit buns Katy had bought from the baker's earlier that afternoon. The weather was quite definitely brightening up.

"You know Mrs. Howard, who takes Science Workshop?" Holly asked, between mouthfuls of bun. "She told us something really amazing. You do know her, don't you? She's always telling us stuff that other teachers don't tell you."

"I certainly do; she taught me science when I was at your school. I was never any good at science, but I loved her lessons," said Katy. "I remember one day she was late getting in to school. When she started our lesson she said, 'Sorry I was a bit late this morning, girls. I got married on Saturday and I've just had my honeymoon.' We all burst out laughing; we thought she was joking, but she wasn't! Anyway, what did she say this afternoon that was so amazing?"

"We were talking about space and time and stuff. She told us that if you look up in the night sky, thousands and thousands of stars you see aren't really there. They burned out hundreds or thousands of years ago! But the light took so long to reach us that we can still see them as they were." Holly paused to finish her bun. "They're so far away that the numbers of miles would be so big that we couldn't write them down. So the distance is measured in light years."

"I once worked out how long a light year is," said Katy. "I did the sum in the sand at low tide with a stick. It took ages. But I do remember that light travels at 186,000 miles per second. I don't know why I didn't just do it on a calculator. I think I just did it for fun."

"I like doing sums," said Beth. "Miss Stewart says I'm the best in my class at sums. You ask me one now; I bet I'll get it right."

"Will everyone shut up and let me tell you about what Mrs. Howard said? Sorry, I don't mean to be rude, but I just want to tell you. I just can't stop thinking about it."

"Just 'cos you're no good at sums," muttered Beth, "you don't want me to show you that I can do them."

"No, Beth, it isn't that. I know you can do them. But please let me tell you. You'll like it, too."

"Oh, all right then. Can I have another bun, Mummy?"

"Okay. This is what she said. She said that if you could be on a star one hundred light years away—I know you can't, but if you could—and you had a very, very, very powerful and clever telescope that could see all that way to earth and the light could reach you instantly, you'd see earth as it was one hundred years ago."

"But you can't," said Beth. "No one's invented a telescope like that. So it's stupid."

"Let Holly go on," said Katy. "I think I know what she's getting at."

"Right. So no one's invented a telescope like that YET. Anyway, the point is that if you could get far enough away, from different places in the galaxy you could see what was happening at all sorts of times in history. Which means whatever happened in the past is still happening. To someone way out in space, that is."

"So the war's still going on and people are still getting beheaded and King Arthur's knights are still killing dragons and things?" A children's magazine had been running a series on famous history stories, and Beth loved it.

"Well, yes, in a way. But the point is," repeated Holly, "that suppose somehow you were somewhere that sort of acted as a telescope all by itself. Don't ask me how, 'cos I don't know. But just suppose it did. Then you could see everything, or even be in it, as it was years and years ago. Don't you think that's terribly exciting? I can't wait for next Science Workshop—Mrs. Howard's going to tell us more about it."

All at once, the sun broke through the clouds and streamed through the kitchen window filling the room with warm, golden light.

"Just look at that!" said Katy. "The weather's clearing up beautifully now. We could go for a walk up on the Downs after tea."

"When are we going to the beach hut again?" asked Beth.

5

It happened again quite suddenly and unexpectedly. The afternoon was warm and sunny, and after so long an absence from the beach, the holidaymakers were out in force. On the most popular stretches of shingle, there was hardly a space between the towels, and those whose bodies were not used to the bright sun were rapidly turning an uncomfortable shade of strawberry pink. The sea was as smooth as glass. Hundreds of people had taken to the water, swimming between the vast array of airbeds and inflatable craft.

Holly, Beth, and her friend Alice were anxious to get in the sea as soon as possible. Holly sat outside the beach hut in an old-fashioned wooden deck chair, the big, comfortable sort with arms which they had been pleased to find at the church fête. She was waiting for the younger girls to get changed into their swimsuits, but there was a lot of giggling going on and every now and then a thump against the doors.

"What are you two *doing?* Whoever's fallen over, get up! Come on, I want to get changed; so does Mum." Holly knocked impatiently on the doors. She had already undone her sandals and tied her hair up in a ponytail and was feeling hot and longing for a swim. Katy was chatting to the people at the next-door hut, whose old golden retriever lay stretched out on the prom in the sun.

"Okay, okay, we're coming!" The doors flew open as Beth and Alice burst into the sunlight, still giggling and struggling to bring a large bright orange inflatable boat with them.

"Hang on, you two!" Katy quickly turned from her chat. "You're not taking that boat out until Holly and I are with you; it's too dangerous, and you'll be lost in the crowd out there. We won't be a minute."

Holly and Katy took their turns in the beach hut to get changed. There really wasn't room for more than two people to change at once.

"Beth, are you still there?" called out Katy from inside. "You are waiting, aren't you?"

There was no answer, just more giggling and shouting, interspersed with a little bark. It seemed that the old dog next door was joining in the fun.

"I don't really trust those two when they get together," said Katy as she hurried to change into her swimsuit. "I know Beth wouldn't be so daft as to go off without one of us, but Alice is overexcited and anything might happen. I'd better go after them quickly." She slipped on her flip-flops and opened one of the doors. "We'll go in near the place where the rescue boat is hauled up on the beach, but we'll wait for you there. Is that okay?"

"Yes, of course. You go, I won't be a minute."

Katy went outside, shutting the door behind her. Holly could hear her calling out: "Wait, you two! Wait just there by the wall, I'm coming!"

She finished changing and put her watch and bracelet into a bag which she hid in the box bench and was just about to go out when she remembered her anklet, a thin gold chain her friend Amy had given her last birthday. She'd nearly lost it once in the sea. Holly sat on the bench and leaned down to undo the clasp of the chain.

It suddenly seemed very much quieter. Perhaps almost everyone was on the beach now instead of charging round the prom getting hot. She had just taken off the anklet when she noticed a folded piece of white paper on the floor. It was funny she hadn't seen it before, she thought. She picked it up, leaned back on the bench, and unfolded it.

It was a note neatly written in pencil in a child's handwriting. It was addressed to 'Holly and Beth, The Beach Hut, Brighton, England, Europe, The World, The Universe.' The message was in French. It read: *Je suis en la plage avec le petit chien Pierre et mes amis. Tous aussi? A bientot, Marjorie xxxxx.* Holly stared at the note, a shiver of excitement running down her spine. She translated the note quietly to herself: "I am on the beach with the little dog Peter and my friends. You also? See you soon, Marjorie."

Could it really have happened again? No, not now; surely not without Beth.

She read it again, turned it over in her hands and flattened it out on the little table, staring at it and feeling the paper. It didn't *feel* old. But then she supposed it wouldn't, not if…

But wait! Was it really a note from Marjorie? Perhaps Beth was playing a trick on her; that was much more likely, except that Beth didn't know that much French.

. *This is silly,* she thought. *Why am I wasting time like this?* She folded the note once more, placed it on the table under a mug and, feeling slightly shaky, went to open the door.

The prom was nearly deserted. How strange it seemed after all the crowds and noise that she had left behind. Yet could she really have returned to 1914? She wondered whether her mother would find the note under the mug; would it still be there in 2001? She didn't even know on which day of the week or even in which year she had arrived. Marjorie was nowhere to be seen. Maybe it wasn't 1914 anymore and maybe she wouldn't be able to find her. The thought crossed Holly's mind that she should go straight back inside the beach hut and close the doors. Just for a moment, she felt afraid. She did so wish that Beth were with her!

The sun was almost overhead and there was hardly a cloud in the sky, but a stiff breeze made the air feel quite cool. Holly rubbed her arms to get warm, wishing she'd picked up her fleece she'd left on the box bench. But what would happen if she did go back inside? No, this was the chance of an adventure, and she couldn't risk losing it.

All the flags were flying on the West Pier, and she could just make out the figures of holidaymakers as they hung on to their hats, the ladies holding their skirts against the wind. And then Holly saw her, a small figure in the distance, running towards her. But wait—she wasn't running; she was dancing! Marjorie's joyful dance steps and the wind blowing her brown hair all over the place made Holly want to laugh out loud with happiness and relief.

"You've come back!" Marjorie was breathless as she pirouetted her last few steps towards Holly. "I knew you would. You found my note, didn't you? But where's Beth? Isn't she with you?" Marjorie collapsed onto the low wall, trying in vain to tie up her hair with the long blue ribbon that had come undone, what with the wind and all her dancing.

"Oh, er, Mummy had to take her somewhere just now. She's got a friend staying. They wanted to go and buy something at the shops."

It sounded a very unlikely excuse, but Marjorie accepted it with a nod. "Maybe she'll come when they've finished shopping," she said. "I do hope so."

Then she was on her feet again, this time holding out the skirt of her navy serge dress as if in a curtsey. "Look! I'm going to show you the new steps I've learned so you can have a try. Oh, just a minute, I must wave to Mother so she knows I'm not lost. Look, there she is near the bandstand, watching us. You wave, too. That's all right, she's seen us."

Marjorie resumed her position, took a step to the right, made a little jump and pointed her left toe forwards. "I love dancing. I wish I could dance and dance and dance all day!"

She was off again, twirling round, pointing her toes and performing more little jumps. "That is, when I'm not bathing in the sea, or taking Peter for a walk, or playing with my cousins." She laughed. "Do you know, I often dream of dancing. I'm in a big, big hall—like the Balham Assembly rooms—and there are mirrors all round, and an orchestra, and I dance so fast my feet hardly touch the ground. Like this!"

Marjorie twirled round and round until she became quite giddy and nearly fell over. She sat down on the wall laughing, but her feet were still tapping as if she could hear the orchestra of her dreams. "Do you like dancing too?" she asked Holly.

"I used to do it when I was younger, but I'm not very good. Beth's brilliant, though. She really loves it. She's learning modern dance now. Mummy and Daddy bought her a karaoke machine for her last birthday, and she sings and dances to it. She bought herself a purple lycra catsuit in a sale at Tammy Girl and—"

"What's a... a... thingamajig, a carrotty machine? You do say funny things sometimes. You're always using words I don't understand. But I don't mind; I like learning new words. It's like learning French."

"Oh—" Holly tried not to laugh. She'd learned a lot from her frequent visits to the museum during the last two weeks so she said, "Well, a karaoke machine is a sort of...a sort of gramophone. It plays different CDs. I mean records, and...well, you can sing along with it." She looked anxiously at Marjorie; she wasn't sure whether she'd said the right thing.

"Oh, we've got a gramophone. I love it. I'm allowed to wind it up sometimes. It's fun to sit right by the big horn, isn't it? It's so loud! Peter gets all excited when we play it; he jumps up and down barking.

What's a catsuit? I saw a pantomime once called 'Puss in Boots' and the cat wore a suit in that. Is it like that? And what's Tammy Girl?"

"Well, kind of, er, not really. Look your mother's waving to us again. Hadn't we better go and meet her?" Holly was pleased to see a way out of further explanations. They ran along the prom together hand in hand, Marjorie now clutching the long blue hair ribbon that had refused to stay in place.

Soon, they were on the beach with Dulcie and Josh and several of their friends. There were two small tents pitched side by side, which seemed to be used as changing rooms, and down by the water's edge was what looked like a small hut on wheels, with steps leading down from the far side into the water. Holly recognised it from photos in the museum as a bathing machine.

"Can we go in there?" Holly pointed to it. "I've never been in a bathing machine," she said, much to the amusement of the other children.

"What do you mean, you've never been in one?" Josh laughed in a kindly way. "I thought you lived here. You're pulling our legs, aren't you? Next time, you'll be telling us you've never had a donkey ride or been on the helter-skelter!"

"Oh no, I have been on a helter-skelter. There's one on the Palace Pier. It's just that…" Holly began.

"You've been on another planet. Don't worry; we know you're joking. But I shall be your guide. We'll pretend you don't know what a bathing machine is. Come along now, Miss Randall." Josh took one hand, and Marjorie and Dulcie took the other. "We will give you a tour of our bathing machine."

The door creaked a little as they opened it. Holly was aware of the tickly feel of sand on the damp wooden floor and the slightly salty, slightly musty smell within.

"Miss Randall," said Josh, with a low bow, "here is our palace, the bathing machine. You see the wheels? A horse would have pulled it down here this morning, when the tide was right. And now," he said, as he opened the door onto the steps, "you have a fine view of the English Channel. To the left, the view is to the West Pier. Please note the English ladies and gentlemen taking their recreation on this fine afternoon. Let us now walk down the steps and put our feet into the water." Josh jumped down into the shallow water and was soon splashing the girls, who followed him in, splashing him in return.

Later, they were sitting on the steps of the bathing machine when Josh became quite serious and solemn.

"Perhaps we won't be able to do this much longer now war's been declared. Mother and Father are worried about what's going to happen. My brother wants to join up, but he's only seventeen so they probably won't let him. I think you have to be eighteen. I'd join up if I was older; I want to fight Kaiser Bill!"

Just for a moment, a shadow fell over the little party. With a shock, Holly began to remember what she had learned in history only last term. She thought of the thousand upon thousand of soldiers who had been killed at Mons and Ypres and the Battle of the Somme; of the mustard gas, the dreadful trenches where so many died. She thought of the film they'd been shown of the devastation that was Flanders Fields, of the dead horses and the countless rows of graves. Three quarters of a million British soldiers had died, she'd learned, and hundreds of thousands horribly wounded. Altogether, ten million people had perished.

She wanted to tell them, but she knew she couldn't. They'd think she was a witch or something, or that she was making it up. She wanted to say to Josh, "Don't let your brother join up—he'll be killed!" Then she remembered how the women had given out white feathers in the streets for cowardice to the young men who wouldn't fight, and she knew she couldn't do it. She couldn't change history but somehow she'd become part of it.

For a brief second, Holly felt dizzy. The sea, the children, everything looked slightly out of focus. No one seemed to notice, and she quickly recovered herself, aware that Josh was still talking. It didn't make sense, on this bright, happy afternoon, to think of war and death. None of it made sense.

"Do you know what they're fighting about?" said Dulcie. "My father says it will all be over by Christmas. I'm getting cold."

"All right," said Josh, springing to his feet. "We'd better go, but I'm going to ask you a joke. If Lord Kitchener and the Kaiser were locked in a car together, who would get out first?"

"We don't know," said Marjorie. "Who would get out first?"

"Lord Kitchener, because he had the car key. Khaki? Do you get it?"

This struck Dulcie as hilariously funny, and she broke into one of her fits of giggles.

Back on the beach, they were grateful for the hot mugs of tea Marjorie's mother had provided. The wind was quite cold now, although the sun was still bright and high. They were sitting in one of the changing tents to keep warm, Peter curled up beside them, when a girl of about fourteen years old appeared at the tent entrance. She was wearing a blue and white striped blouse with a big square collar over a long, navy blue skirt. She was holding the straw hat Holly had worn when they had been playing trenches. Her shoulder-length, crinkly ginger hair was tied in a bunch at the back, and she had smiling, grey eyes flecked with gold.

"Oh hello, Amelia," said Josh, pushing his hair back and smoothing down his bathing suit. "Are you coming to join us?"

"No, I've come to tell you that Aunty Lily says it's time to go home. I've got your clothes here. The girls can have the other tent; I'm all ready."

Dulcie leaned conspiratorially towards Holly and Marjorie. "Josh has got a pash on Amelia," she whispered.

§ § § § §

How the afternoon had flown by! Holly helped pack up the picnic and the tents and held one handle of the big heavy beach bag as they struggled up the shingle to the prom. As she was saying goodbye and beginning to walk back towards the beach hut, Marjorie ran after her.

"I forgot to tell you—it's Daddy's birthday today. He's coming down on the train from London, and we're all going to meet him at the railway station. We're going to have a party for him at Josh's father's hotel."

"Oh, have a lovely time!" said Holly, "Say Happy Birthday to him from me. What day is it today? I've forgotten."

"It's August 5th, of course! The war started yesterday. Oh, and you know what Vera said on the beach last time you came, about Austria and Serbia? Mother says that was very important. I'm going to remember it for ever and ever."

"Yes, I think I will, too." Holly was quite sure she would. "I'd better go now, or I shall be late getting back."

"Come again soon. Come tomorrow. Bring Beth with you. Tell her to bring her cat costume. Bring your mother, then she can meet my mother so she won't be worried if you stay longer. We've got to go home on Saturday and we may not be back for ages and ages. It's Wednesday today, so we've only got two more days. You *must* come; please say you'll come!"

"We'll try. I want to come so much." *More than you could ever guess,* thought Holly. "It might not actually be tomorrow, but we'll really try."

6

Fearing she might be late, Holly began to run the few hundred yards along the prom when she remembered she need not worry at all. Time would have moved on only a few minutes in 2001. As she reached the first of the row of beach huts, she noticed a short, stocky man in a striped blazer with a camera on a tripod. Sitting in front of him, on a rather rickety looking chair, sat a small boy with a monkey on his shoulder. The monkey was dressed in a red and white suit and had a fez on his head. A lady—Holly guessed it was the boy's mother—was standing next to the photographer and encouraging her son to smile at the camera.

"That's right, sonny," said the photographer, "you 'old that smile 'o yours just like that, and we'll 'ope that Alfie there be'aves 'imself on your shoulder. 'Ere goes then."

He ducked under a big black cloth for what seemed a long time, but the monkey kept still. The little boy's smile was beginning to fade when there was flash and a small bang and the photographer emerged triumphant.

"Well done, sonny. You've got a grand little lad there, lady," he said, turning to the boy's mother. She smiled and put some money in his hand.

Then the photographer noticed Holly. "'Ow would you like your picture taken, missy? Alfie's all ready for another customer."

"Oh, er, I can't," said Holly, "I haven't got any money with me and..."

"Don't you worry about that, missy. You can pay me when you picks up the photograph. It'll be ready tomorrow. If you don't come back tomorrow, I hangs it up on the wall 'ere, see, and you picks it up next time you're passing. I'm 'ere every afternoon in 'oliday time if it ain't rainin'."

Holly was about to refuse again when an idea came to her. "All right," she said, "but can you turn the chair round so that the West Pier's in the background? And, please, could we ask someone to be in the picture with me?"

"Well, well, missy, I don't see why I shouldn't oblige. You take care of Alfie."

He put the little monkey carefully on Holly's shoulder. She was glad that Marjorie's mother had suggested she borrow a shawl for her walk back; even still, the little animal felt quite uncomfortable. Then he leaned sideways and looked at her with his bright black eyes and carefully removed his hat with one paw and did a little bow to her. Holly laughed.

"I see you got our Alfie trained already!" said the photographer. "Now, let's just try you sitting down 'ere." Holly carefully sat down on the old chair, anxious that the monkey did not slip. "That's it. We got the pier right in view. Now, we just got to get you a companion, 'ain't we?" He looked around at the passers-by. A young woman in a high-necked white blouse, a long green skirt, and a pretty straw hat with a green ribbon had stopped to watch. "Ah, madam, would you kindly oblige and pose with me young friend 'ere? She don't want to be alone with our Alfie." He gave Holly a wink.

"Oh, well, yes, I'll join the little girl. I'm, well, I'm not very good with, um, animals," she gave a nervous laugh, "but I'll look after the young lady." She turned to Holly. "Don't worry, he won't bite you." She smiled and gave Holly a little pat on the shoulder.

"Say cheese now, ladies." The photographer disappeared once more under the black cloth and Holly waited for the bang. She understood how the little boy had had trouble holding his smile; it seemed a long wait.

"All done, ladies," he said, "We should 'ave a good'un there!"

§ § § § §

Holly skipped along the prom. A plan was beginning to form in her mind, but it was not quite clear yet. There was still the problem of how to pay for the photo. She had no idea where she would find any old money; it had been out of circulation for thirty years.

The events and conversations of the day were still crowding in on her when she realised that she'd come to the end of the row of beach huts. She'd been so lost in her thoughts that she must have passed by her own without noticing. She turned to retrace her steps and then noticed something she had not noticed before: during the afternoon, several of the beach huts had been given a new coat of paint. Then she remembered seeing the painter's brushes and pots of paint neatly stacked in a wooden box somewhere, presumably waiting to be collected.

A moment of awful panic, which had Holly's heart beating far too fast, was replaced by relief when she spotted the familiar red doors some half dozen huts down. She ran back, clutching the cream woollen shawl round her, but when she got there the doors were locked. A shiny new padlock held the clasp tightly in place.

Holly stared in disbelief and horror. She seized the padlock and tried to wrench it open. She shook it and pulled at the doors. The bolt in the floor on the right hand side was fast in place; the doors would not budge an inch.

The strange feeling that Holly had had in the bathing machine came over her again. She began to feel dizzy and the prom swam before her eyes in a shimmering haze. She sat down on the wooden step with her head in her hands, thinking all the time: "I've got to recover myself. I've got to think what to do. Will I be stuck here forever in the wrong time? It'll get dark, and I've nowhere to go. What will I *do?*"

She felt as if her head would explode. People passed by, but no one seemed to notice her.

After a few moments, she found that the dizziness was beginning to pass. She managed to stand up, and she banged on the doors.

"Mummy! Beth! Let me in! Please, let me in!" There was no reply. No sound at all came from within.

It was quite illogical, of course. The beach hut was locked from the outside, but Holly couldn't be logical. It was all too frightening. She banged again on the door. "Let me in! *Please* let me in!"

This time, an elderly couple stopped. The woman showed great concern and put her arm round Holly, who by now was almost overcome by dizziness again and beginning to cry.

"There, there, dear. Don't cry, we'll help you. Have you lost your mother? You just tell us where you live, and we'll see you home." They were being very kind; the elderly gentleman brought over a deckchair which had been left by the wall and helped Holly to sit down.

"You don't understand!" Holly sobbed, "I don't live here. I mean, I do live in Brighton, but…but…oh, it's no good. You couldn't understand. No one could." She tried to get up, but the kindly lady took her hands and pulled her down again.

"I was a nurse in my younger days and I can see you need to sit still for a while or you'll come over dizzy again. Edwin," she turned to her husband, "get the young lady a drink of water. Here's a cup." She took a blue and white china teacup from her picnic bag. "And there's the tap just over there. That's right, by the wall. Now," she turned back to Holly and sat down on the steps next to her, "what's your name, dear?"

"Holly. Holly Randall. But I must go and find my friends!" She tried to get up again, but soon realised that it was hopeless. "Oh no, I can't. They've gone to the railway station. Maybe if I go to the railway station…"

"Now, if they went to the railway station, they would most probably have taken a cab or an omnibus. It's too far to walk from here. I think it would be very difficult for you to find your friends. But anyway, you tell me all about it. I'm Mrs. Johnston, Esther Johnston, and this is my husband, Edwin. Ah, thank you, Edwin." She took the cup of water from her husband and held it for Holly to drink. The coldness of it cleared her head a little. "Is that better now? Let's wrap this lovely warm shawl round you and then you can tell me all about it." Mrs. Johnston spoke soothingly. She had twinkling blue eyes and dimples in her rather plump cheeks.

Holly was shivering. She hadn't noticed the shawl had slipped from her shoulders, and it was now quite late in the afternoon and getting colder. "I do live in Brighton," Holly began, "but you won't be able to find my mother. She's—" she paused, desperately trying to think what to say next.

"Oh, my dear, I'm so sorry." Mrs. Johnston looked most concerned. "Did she pass on recently? Perhaps your father…"

"No, no, she's not dead. She's… she's…" Holly could think of no way of explaining except the truth. "She's…well, she's in the future. I've come from the future. I live with my mother and father and sister Beth, and it's 2001 in our time and…"

Mrs. Johnston put her hand on Holly's forehead. "I think you're a little feverish, my dear. All right, you come from the future," she gave her husband a wink. "Tell me about your friends. Are they from the future, too?" She sounded like a schoolmistress addressing a class of small children.

"Oh no, they live here now," said Holly. "I met Marjorie in this beach hut, and I met her cousins and friends on the beach and…" she was beginning to feel dizzy again, but she had to go on, "they were talking about the war. It's going to go on for four years! I wanted to tell them, but I couldn't. I don't know what to do."

"You just sit still for a moment or two, Holly dear. That's right, have another little sip of water."

Mrs. Johnston stood up, took her husband's arm, and walked a few paces away, but Holly could still hear what they were saying. "Edwin, I think the young girl's not very well. She may be coming down with something. There's scarlet fever in the area, I've heard. I think it's best we get the policeman from by the pier to take her details in case her mother is looking for her, and then we must get her home just as soon as possible."

"Right ho, my love. You always know best." Edwin nodded in agreement. "Yes, we'll hire a cab and try to get her home."

They went on talking, Mrs. Johnston glancing back at Holly from time to time. It occurred to Holly to run away. But where would she go? She didn't know the name of the hotel owned by Josh's father where Marjorie and her parents would be staying. She didn't even know Josh's surname, or Marjorie's or Dulcie's.

Just as tears were beginning to well up in Holly's eyes once more, a man in paint-splattered overalls came over and stood in front of her.

"'Scuse me, miss. I'm awful sorry to bother you, miss, but you're sitting in front of me box of paints and brushes. Could you oblige by moving forward an inch or two?"

Holly looked dazed for a moment. "Oh yes. Yes, of course." She began to pull the deck chair forward.

"Very kind of you, miss, I'm sure."

He picked up the wooden box Holly had seen earlier, and a smaller box which had been behind it. It was strange she had not noticed they were there when she'd been banging on the doors.

"'Ere they are. And 'ere's me box o' numbers. I 'ad to take off the numbers, you see, to make a good job of it, but I've got me plan all here so I knows what's what. You sit still, miss. I'm all right now."

"What did you say?" Holly sat up straight. Something seemed to catch in her throat and her voice sounded dry. "Did you say numbers? You took the numbers off? All the numbers?"

"As I was saying, miss, you 'ave to, to do a good job. Are you all right, miss? You look awful peculiar."

"No, no, I'm fine." She was surprised to see that Mr. and Mrs. Johnston were still deep in conversation. She had to move fast before they came back. She stood up, still feeling a little shaky.

"Can you tell me," she asked the painter, "is this the only beach hut in this row you haven't painted today?"

"Yes, miss. The owners were 'ere all day. They didn't want no wet paint to contend with. Are you sure you're all right, miss? You'd best sit down again. I got a little lass just a bit younger than you, and she comes over funny sometimes wi' too much sun. Maybe you've been out in the sun too much?"

"No, no, honestly, I'm fine. Please, this is really important. Did you paint another hut which had red doors?"

"Let me think. Yes, now you comes to mention it, I'm quite sure I did. But I'll just check me little list. I've been right busy today, it's hard to remember them all."

He pulled a crumpled piece of paper from his pocket and a pair of reading glasses, somewhat flecked with paint. "Yes, 'ere we are. Lucky I ain't lost this list or I wouldn't know where to put all them numbers, would I? Right, count four huts down towards the pier and you'll see a yellow hut with bright blue doors. Paint should be dry by now. Come to think of it, I remember that one in particular, like, 'cos them doors were open and no one was in."

"Thank you! Oh, thank you!" To the painter's astonishment, Holly flung her arms round him and ran.

Just as she reached the bright blue doors, she saw Mrs. Johnston hurrying towards her.

"It's all right, dear! We'll have you home in no time. Edwin has gone for help." She was now almost beside Holly, who stepped smartly into the beach hut.

"Thank you, I won't be a moment," Holly called out as she pulled the doors shut behind her.

There were the familiar yellow box benches and the mugs and the biscuit tin. There were Beth's clothes on the floor where she'd left them, and there was her own brightly coloured beach towel with the sea horses on it, hanging on a hook on the wall.

Holly sat down on a bench and closed her eyes. She found herself praying out loud, "Oh please, God, let it be 2001. Please, God, let it be 2001," over and over again.

She felt it in her toes first, the warmth from the sunlight as it streamed under the doors. Then the noise struck her, the shouting and laughter and a radio playing next door. In a few seconds, she was out on the hot crowded beach, weaving her way through the sunbathers and picnickers. There was the rescue boat and—oh joy!—there was her mother with Beth and Alice.

"I love you, Mummy!" she said, flinging her arms round her mother now. "And I love you, Beth. I love you too, Alice. I've missed you so much. I love, I love you, I love you!"

Katy laughed. "We've only been waiting a few minutes." She looked rather puzzled. "Still, it's nice to be appreciated. Come on, let's get this boat launched."

They worked their way through the crowds of children paddling at the sea's edge and then the orange dinghy was free of the beach, bobbing in the waist-high water. Alice scrambled in first.

Beth turned to Holly, a look of suspicion on her face. She could keep up the pretence no longer. "You've been there, haven't you? You've been there without me. That's not fair!"

7

Holly's experience had shocked and frightened her. She woke several times in the night and turned on the light to reassure herself that she was still in her own time. Once, she crept into Beth's bedroom, but Beth was fast asleep under her Barbie duvet, surrounded by her toys and Top 20 Chart posters.

In spite of Holly's fright, or maybe even because of it, she was longing to be back in that time so long ago when Britain was on the brink of a war, the likes of which had never been seen before and would change the whole of Europe for ever. The horror of what she'd learned at school about the terrible battles, the trench warfare and all those deaths haunted her. Yet she could hardly wait to see Marjorie and her cousins again. It was strange; she felt as if she'd known Marjorie all her life, just as if she were a little sister, like Beth. And what was even stranger, Marjorie seemed to accept her as part of the family.

There were so many questions in Holly's mind. Who were they all, Marjorie and her cousins and friends? Why had she and Beth come into their world just when they did? Was Josh's father's hotel still on the seafront and—though she was not sure she wanted to know the answer to this—had Josh's brother joined up? Did he survive the war or was he among the endless lists of war dead? There seemed to be trails going off all over the place, trails she wanted to follow.

Then she began to wonder whether she and Beth would be able to go farther than the beach on their next visit. There must be a next visit, there just had to be. How wonderful it would be if they—for surely Beth would be with her next time—could actually go on the West Pier and see it as it was in its heyday!

She thought about how, that evening, Beth had owned up to her that she'd lied to their mother about not being with her when they stepped out of the beach hut into 1914. Although Beth was only nine years old, she liked to be in control of a situation, and how could she be when things were happening that she didn't understand? It wasn't possible, and therefore, it could not have happened. People can't just suddenly go back eighty-seven years in time simply by opening a perfectly ordinary door. But she and Holly did, and now Holly had gone on her own and it just wasn't fair.

Eventually, Holly fell into a deep, dreamless sleep, only to be wakened by their cat, Sooty, pouncing onto her bed and trying to crawl under the duvet.

The morning dawned grey and dull. "Typical of good old England," their father muttered as he was getting ready to leave for work. "I suppose yesterday was all the summer we're going to get. Perhaps your mother's right, girls; we should go away somewhere where it stays hot and sunny. I'll see what I can arrange. It's a bit quieter now at the Garden Centre, so it should be possible. Anyway, you two have a good day. Doesn't look much like beach weather."

He gave them a wave as he set off down the drive on his bike. Stephen Randall owned the Garden Centre as his father and grandfather had done before him, although in those days it was Randall's Dahlia Nurseries and famous throughout the south of England.

"I hope Daddy won't arrange anything too soon," Holly whispered anxiously to Beth.

After breakfast, Katy drove the girls into town. It was Beth's dancing class and, as it was to be the dress rehearsal for the show they were performing that evening, the class would be longer than usual.

"Would you like to come shopping with me, Holly?" asked her mother as they pulled away from the church hall where the class was held. "Or I could drop you off at the Garden Centre and you could give Daddy a hand."

"No, it's okay. I've got some work to do at the museum on my project. Can you meet me there when you've finished shopping?"

§ § § § §

The museum was quiet and peaceful after all the heavy holiday traffic. Holly stopped by the giant cat for a moment and looked for a coin in her purse. She fed it to him and was rewarded with the growly "thank you" she loved to hear.

Mr. Edwards's office was just along the corridor. She did so much hope he'd be in; she needed his help this morning. She knocked on the door, but there was no reply. Disappointed, she tried his secretary's office next door.

"Yes, he's here," said Miss Jones, hardly taking her eyes off the computer screen. "You'll find him upstairs somewhere. Try the costume gallery."

Holly hurried up the stairs. She had just over an hour and no time to lose. She spotted Mr. Edwards in his familiar tweed suit and shiny brown shoes talking to a small boy and his mother by the Elizabethan Room. Holly would have to wait until they had finished talking, but she purposefully walked round to the other side of the Elizabethan Room so he would see her. He did, and he gave her a little wave.

"Good morning, young lady," said Mr. Edwards when the small boy and his mother had moved on to the next room. "How's the project going? You were waiting to see me."

"Yes, I want to ask you something. It's about the First World War. Can you tell me anything about what happened here in Brighton? I really need to see some photos and old newspapers and things."

"Well, now, we have a gallery through here," he beckoned Holly to follow him, "just waiting for your attention. Is there anything in particular you would like to know? Now, here's something which might interest you."

He led her to a display case full of sepia photographs of Brighton's Royal Pavilion. Alongside the photographs were letters and newspaper cuttings. But the Pavilion looked very different from how Holly knew it. The grand staterooms were full of beds in which were lying wounded soldiers.

"Yes, the Royal Pavilion became the Indian Hospital during the Great War. Special trains ran into Brighton station carrying the wounded," explained Mr. Edwards. "I'm afraid many died of their wounds, but they had excellent care here. This photograph was taken late in 1914. Is this the sort of thing you wanted to see?"

"Yes, oh yes, it is." Holly wasn't sure how to go on. She wanted to tell him, but she couldn't seem to find the right words. So she said, "You see, I've…well, I've been there."

"Of course you have, young Holly. I should think almost everyone in Brighton has been to the Royal Pavilion, but they would not have seen it like this."

"No, I don't mean that. I mean I've…oh dear, this is going to sound really silly! I've been to 1914. We were in the beach hut, Beth and I were, and it just sort of happened."

"Ah." Mr. Edwards looked very serious, but also rather excited. "I think we should have a little chat. Come and sit down, and tell me all about it."

He led the way to a comfortable looking dark red, buttoned-back leather sofa at the far end of an adjacent gallery "We shouldn't be disturbed too much here," he said.

They sat down side by side, Holly feeling a little embarrassed.

"You didn't sound surprised," she said. "I thought you'd think I was making it up."

"No. No, definitely not. You see," Mr. Edwards lowered his voice, "it happened to me once."

Holly could hardly believe her ears. She was so excited she wanted to shout and scream and dance round the gallery, but she sat still and tried to keep calm. "You mean you went back to 1914, too? Through a beach hut?"

"No, with me it happened at a railway station, and it was 1876. But I can see that you're longing to tell me about your adventure, so I'll just sit here and listen."

"Oh, please tell me what happened to you. I want to know first. That is, if you don't mind."

"Very well, then. I'll give you a little of my story and then you can tell me yours. I'm afraid no one believed me at the time, nor have they ever since, not even my own parents or brothers. They have always been convinced I fell asleep and that my experience was nothing but a dream. But now here we are, fellow time travellers. I never thought I'd see the day. This is just wonderful!" Mr. Edwards gave her a beaming smile before continuing with his story.

"It happened in 1964. Dr. Beeching had started his dreadful programme the year before to close down over two thousand small railway stations across Britain. It was July 17th; it was a Friday, and the summer term had just ended. I was on my way home from school for the last time."

"How old were you?" Holly didn't think he'd mind her asking.

"It was my eighteenth birthday that very day. There was quite a crowd of us on Upper Winterbourne station. All the boys from school and many others. Our train was to be the last one that would ever run on that line; the station was closing that very evening."

"Everyone must have been very sad." Holly looked thoughtful.

"Indeed we were. Upper Winterbourne was such a pretty station. It had served our school ever since the railway had been built. Queen Victoria herself had been at the opening ceremony. There were some wonderful photographs in the waiting room. Her Majesty looked very sombre, of course; she wore only black, you know, after her beloved Albert died."

"So how did it happen? Did it happen just to you?"

"Yes, I was the only one. We were just standing talking, fooling around a bit, I'm afraid. Some of the chaps were sitting on their luggage. There was a big crowd of us, as I said. Anyway, we had a while to wait, and I was thirsty. I went into the little station buffet for a bottle of Tizer. Can you still buy Tizer? "

"I'm not sure. I think so," Holly said.

"We loved it; it was very popular. Anyway, when I'd finished my drink, I opened the old frosted glass doors onto the platform. My friends had gone. All our luggage had gone. At first I thought I'd missed the train, but there were still a lot of people on the platform. But they weren't the people I'd left behind. And the light was different. Yes, the light was definitely different. The scene was just a little out of focus, but it soon became clear."

"That's what happened to me and Beth!" interrupted Holly. "It was just like that. Oh please, do go on."

"Well, of course, then I recognised it from the old photograph in the waiting room. My late afternoon in July had become an autumn morning. The leaves on the trees were turning to gold, and there was a heavy dew on the geraniums in the window boxes. Deep pink geraniums, they were. Do you know, if I shut my eyes, I can still almost feel the dampness of the cold, clear air. There must have been a ground frost during the night because the distant hills were white where the sun had not yet touched them. But what struck me most was the brightness of the shining rails and the smell of the newly painted woodwork on the station buildings. The doors were all glossy dark green with brass fittings. And the clock. The clock was enormous! I remember watching the second hand as it moved around the dial and listening to the rhythmic tick. It was five minutes to nine when I arrived.

"I must have looked rather lost because a middle-aged couple with a small Yorkshire terrier on a plaited leather lead befriended me. The lady wore a long, brown fur-edged coat and had a muff round her neck of the same material for warming her hands. There was a scent of mothballs about her, and I remember wondering if she'd got out this rather splendid outfit especially for the Queen's visit, for I didn't doubt it was that very day. She had a hat to match too, and she wore jet earrings; the black shiny stones caught the sunlight as we were talking. Her husband wore a black frock coat and a grey top hat which was a little large for him. It reminded me of the Mad Hatter's hat in Alice in Wonderland. I remember thinking, mercifully not out loud, that there should be a label stuck in the ribbon with 10/6d written on it! They introduced themselves as Mr. and Mrs. Enoch Jameson." Mr. Edwards paused, shutting his eyes for a moment as he pictured the long forgotten scene.

"Memory's a strange thing you know, Holly. People you've met, things you've seen and done, can remain hidden for years in the deep recesses of your mind, forgotten to all intents and purposes, maybe because they are not needed at the time. Then some small thing can trigger them, open the door to them, so to speak, and they'll come flooding back in. It is, of course," he continued with a smile, "very useful when, you're trying to revise for an exam, to know that nothing is ever really forgotten."

"It seems to be for me," said Holly with a grin. "Please, go on."

"Well now, we were standing there talking for quite a little while. Mrs. Jameson said she recognised my school tie. She said, 'We have great hopes, don't we, my dear,' addressing her husband who nodded vigorously, 'that our little lad, our grandson, Arthur, will be able to go to your school in a few years' time.' Then suddenly a hush fell on the chattering crowd. I could hear the singing in the silver rails and in the far distance puffs of smoke were rising above the trees. But now, Holly, I'd like to hear your story."

"Oh, Mr. Edwards, please don't end there!" Holly pleaded. There was so much she wanted to know, although she was longing to tell him about her own experience. Here was someone who would really understand, who'd done the same unbelievable thing she and Beth had done.

"I'll stop there because," said Mr. Edwards, "there is more to tell, and it's important that I hear your story. I can see it's bursting to be told."

In the corner of the gallery where Holly sat with Mr. Edwards on the red leather sofa, the telling of her tale interrupted only occasionally with his brief questions or murmurs of encouragement, a small party of children sat on the floor with clipboards in hand. A young woman, smartly dressed, was speaking to them in French. Some of them were busy writing, others drawing, quite unaware of the extraordinary conversation going on between the dark-haired girl with the long baggy jeans and the curator of the museum.

Just one little boy in a lime-green shell suit and a black Nike baseball cap whose attention had lapsed turned to stare at them. He was chewing the end of his pencil and held his clipboard over his head. But Ma'mselle, his teacher, spotted him.

"Louis! Attention, *s'il vous plait!*"

The boy turned away from observing Holly, who was just demonstrating to Mr. Edwards the monkey's comic movement as he took off his fez to her and bowed. As Holly was coming to the end of her story, a clock downstairs struck the hour. Twelve loud, resonant chimes echoed through the building. It drew Holly back sharply to the present day.

"Oh no!" she cried, jumping up. "My mother's going to be here any minute. I'd better go downstairs and wait for her. We've got to pick up Beth."

"The clock is a little fast, but we certainly mustn't keep your mother waiting. Have you told your parents about your experience?"

"I told Mummy, but I'm not sure if she believed me. She did think it was odd, though, about the sandy footprints Mr. Jim saw in the beach hut. I don't think Daddy would understand. He'd like to but, well, you know. It sounds so sort of like a fairy story."

"You should tell them anyway. Perhaps, like me, you may never be believed, but it's good for the story to be told, at least to those close to you. You know, Holly," said Mr. Edwards as they walked back through the gallery, "there's nothing magical about your experience. There's not some touchstone that will make it happen. There's nothing ghostly, either. I believe we have both been granted this privilege of a door into the past for a special reason, even though that reason may not yet be clear at all. It certainly changed my life. After my experience, I saw history for what it is, not something old and past but part of the present and the future. And now I've made it my life's study."

Soon they were entering the archive gallery where Holly had looked at the old photographs of the Royal Pavilion when it had served as the Indian Hospital in the First World War.

"Don't forget, my dear fellow traveller," Mr. Edwards continued, "you can't change history, however much you may want to. It's more than likely that Josh's brother, for example, did join up and perhaps was killed or injured in the war, and maybe other relatives of the friends you met on the beach. But there's nothing you can do about it.

You certainly can't prevent it, and you mustn't try. You've simply become part of their world for a while. You're there by grace. Always remember that: you're there by grace. Someday, you will discover why. Perhaps tomorrow, or next year, or in fifty years' time."

As they passed the glass case containing the photographs of the Indian soldiers in their beds, Holly paused for a moment to take another look. One picture caught her attention. It was of a nurse standing by the bed of one of the patients; he had a bandage over one eye, and she was apparently adjusting the sling on his injured arm. A caption underneath the picture read: "Nurse Florence Anselm tends one of our wounded heroes."

It was the young woman in the pretty straw hat who had joined Holly in the photograph with the West Pier resplendent in the background.

8

Holly could not get Mr. Edwards's words out of her mind. What did he mean, "you're there by grace"? She wanted to talk to her mother about it on the way back to the church hall to pick up Beth, but the traffic was awful, and Katy had to concentrate hard on avoiding holidaymakers who didn't seem to know the one-way system. Twice, the car in front of them changed lanes amidst hoots from angry drivers. The heavy rain did nothing to help the situation. So Holly said nothing of her conversation with Mr. Edwards. And then there was the photograph of Nurse Anselm. She felt that somehow it was there especially for her, but hard as it was to keep all this to herself, she would have to wait for the right moment when her mother would be able to listen properly.

The show was to start at 7 pm that evening. By 5 pm, Beth was already anxious to be off. She had a starring role in the second half and her artistic temperament was beginning to show itself.

"Come on, everyone—we've got to go! No, I don't want another cup of tea. We've got to GO!"

She was pacing round the kitchen, swinging her carrier bag containing her costume and ballet shoes. She looked up at the clock every few seconds, banged her chair against the table, and then tried to take Holly's beans-on-toast away.

"You can't eat that! We've got to GO! Haven't we, Mummy? Tell her she can't eat it."

"I will not. Calm down, Beth. You haven't got to be there until quarter past six. It's Saturday, it'll only take us about ten minutes to get there. Now, sit down and have your tea. You'll be hungry if you don't, and then you won't dance so well."

Beth stormed up to the table, flung her bag on the floor, and glared at her mother.

"How can I eat at a time like this? Suppose the car won't start? Daddy might've forgotten to put any petrol in it." She pushed her plate away but picked up a chocolate biscuit.

Stephen leaned over and grabbed it from her, pushing the beans-on-toast back in its place. "Beth, the car is full of petrol. I want to see my little princess dance her best. Now, it will be much quicker if you just calm down and eat up. We don't want you to faint on stage."

Beth glared again, grabbed her knife and fork, and attacked her plate of beans-on-toast as if it were a dreaded enemy. Holly, who'd been trying not to laugh, caught Katy's eye just as she was drinking her cup of tea. Almost choking and laughing at the same time, she rushed from the room, her napkin over her face.

"Now look what's happened!" shouted Beth, flinging her knife and fork down, "Holly's going to make us really late. That's it. I can't eat another thing." She leaned back in her chair, arms folded, a defiant look on her face.

Holly reappeared, slightly red in the face, and went to the kitchen sink for a glass of water.

"For goodness sake, Beth!" said Stephen, usually the calm one of the family but now beginning to lose his temper. "If you don't finish your tea, we won't go at all, and someone else will have to take your part."

"Yes, and it will probably be Miranda, and that'll show you," said Holly.

Miranda was Beth's dreaded rival. She always looked neat and tidy and wore her hair pulled back in a tight 'chignon' like professional ballet dancers. She said, "Yes, Miss" whenever she was asked to do anything and was often given a starring role. To say that there was a clash of personalities was putting it mildly.

"Oh no she *won't*! I'd rather DIE than let Miranda have my part!"

Beth picked up her knife and fork again and began to eat. "Okay. Sorry, sorry, sorry, sorry. Please can I have some more tea, Mummy?"

Katy poured her another cup. She picked it up to drink, giving each of them a stare over the rim of the cup, but said not another word until the meal was finished. But there was a rhythmic kick of her trainers against the table leg that somehow everyone managed to ignore. Holly was silently shaking with mirth, but Beth wisely managed to ignore it. Maybe it was the thought of Miranda in *her* costume dancing *her* part.

§ § § § § §

By 6:30 pm, the church hall was already nearly full. Every child who attended the dancing school was to take part, and so almost all the parents had arrived early with their children. Any empty seats had programmes or coats placed on them to reserve them for grandparents, aunts and uncles, and friends. Cushions had been placed right at the front for the smallest children.

St. Hilda's Jubilee Church Hall, built to commemorate Queen Victoria's Diamond Jubilee in 1897, was sadly in need of renovation. The walls showed signs of damp and the yellowing paint was peeling badly high up near the roof. The old night storage heaters, which were covered in wire mesh grills, were beginning to rust, and the floor was pock-marked with small holes from the days of the 1960s when stiletto heels were in fashion. The once grand wine-red velvet curtains were faded brown in places, and the elaborate twirls of gold braid that decorated the edges were tarnished and tattered.

But none of this affected the feeling of excitement and anticipation which was clearly present amidst the waiting audience. There was much shifting of the old wooden chairs as latecomers squeezed down the rows with many a "'scuse me! Oh, sorry!" and "Can I just—yes, that's my seat down there. Thanks a lot."

Miss Anne Rider, who had started the dancing school fifty-four years ago, put her head round the double doors leading out to the corridor and smiled. She was happy to see such a large audience, not only for the sake of her pupils, but also for St. Hilda's Church. All the ticket money was to go to the Church Hall Restoration Fund, a project dear to her heart. She could see it now in her mind's eye: glossy bright paintwork, a gleaming new wooden floor with no fear of splinters for young feet. There would be blue velvet curtains. Yes, blue would go well with the floor, perhaps a bright azure blue with gold tassels on the edges. She just hoped and prayed that she'd still be running the school when this perfection was put in place.

She closed the doors again. *No time for this now,* she thought; *the littlest ones must be getting in line for the first scene.* How she loved her shows! In all the years she'd produced them, she never failed to feel the children's excitement and thrill at a good performance. Whatever went wrong, it was always a good performance. She made sure of that and always praised every child individually. In the old days,

she would think of them as her children; now they were like a large
family of grandchildren. They loved it, and they loved her.

With her snowy white hair held in a loose bun by a number of
combs and pins, and her ample figure, she was frequently described
as 'cuddly.' Tonight, she wore an ankle-length, flared, powder blue
cotton jersey skirt with jacket to match. Her glasses, on a long gold
chain, hung round her neck. She wore a brooch on her jacket in the
shape of a little gold ballerina, a much-loved gift from class one last
year. In her day, she had danced with the Royal Ballet and was proud
to display a photograph of herself with the famous ballerina, Dame
Margot Fonteyn, when they had danced together in 'Swan Lake.' But
a serious knee injury after a fall had ended her career suddenly at the
age of twenty-six. She started the School of Dance the same year, and
in spite of her injury, she could even now perform most of the steps
she taught her pupils.

Katy, Stephen, and Holly had arrived in time to find good seats
near the front. Katy opened her programme. It read:

"Miss Anne Rider's School of Dance

Presents its

54th. Summer Show

Scene One: The Song of the Sea

A wondrous tale of the deep performed by classes 1 and 2"

She was proud to see her younger daughter's name in bold on the
second page under the heading "The Magic Toy Shop." There she
was, at the top of the cast list: "Pop Idol Doll: Elizabeth Randall."

A hush was falling over the audience as the lights were turned out
one by one, leaving only the spot lights positioned on a beam in the
ceiling to shine down on the old velvet curtains. The shifting of feet
and shuffling of programmes were gradually silenced as the music,
under the care of Alice's father, who was a local radio sound techni-
cian, gradually rose and the curtains opened.

The first piece of music was, as it had been for the past fifty-three
years, whatever the subject of the scene, 'The Rustle of Spring.' The
littlest girls, the three to four-year-olds, were dressed in blue and
green silky tunics and represented waves; they held blue and green
ribbons above their heads as they danced and the music gradually
changed to 'Fingall's Cave.' Long strands of seaweed hung from a
screen at the back of the stage, lit up by green and blue spotlights
from the beam.

The slightly older children represented fish and other sea creatures as they moved gracefully around the dancing 'waves'. Then suddenly, one tiny girl, Alice's younger sister, Emily, stepped just a little too near the edge of the stage and fell headlong on to the piled cushions where the smallest children were sitting.

A gasp went up from the audience, but in a matter of seconds, Miss Rider had scooped her up in her arms quite unhurt and popped her back on the stage again with a whispered, "Well done, my poppet. You were a little wave coming ashore. Off you go now!"

There were no tears, and Emily was soon back in step with the others, a little shaky but smiling bravely. There was never anything but professionalism from Miss Anne Rider; the show must always go on.

The seven to eight-year-olds were next, in a dance entitled "The Enchanted Wood." A quick change of scene revealed a tree stump in the middle of the stage and a scattering of leaves on the floor. To the strains of 'Greensleeves', little girls dressed as fairies and elves joined hands as they danced around the tree stump and then, dropping hands, jumped and pirouetted while some clever lighting effected moonlight on the Enchanted Wood.

Holly, who had been in the shows herself until two years before and had watched Beth in her shows, found her attention drifting as she knew none of the girls in this class. But then something made her sit up, almost as if her eyes had opened after a deep sleep. It was the echo of Mr. Edwards's words in her head: "I saw history for what it is, not something old and past but part of the present and the future." Marjorie could be any one of the older girls in this class. Didn't she tell Holly, "I love dancing. I wish I could dance and dance all day"? Didn't she say that she dreams of dancing? On their last afternoon together on the beach, Marjorie had told Holly how her mother had made her costumes for her dancing shows. She too had been a fairy with a short tulle dress and silver wings and wore silk flowers in her hair. Her mother had made her a Welsh costume and a Country Girl costume. "Mother's very clever," she had told Holly. "She makes *lovely* clothes. Sometimes she makes them for Dulcie, too. I hope I can sew like Mother when I grow up."

If Marjorie had come on to the stage now dressed in her fairy costume, Holly would have hardly been surprised. It would have been quite right, just as it should be. She'd be pointing her toes and pirouetting with the others, just as she'd done on the prom, and Miss Rider would love her.

Holly was disturbed from her thoughts by the tumultuous applause that marked the end of the first half and the stampede for refreshments served from a hatch at the back of the hall. Several of her friends from school were there, and she spotted Jessica near the front of the queue. Holly pushed her way through, taking care to avoid grown-ups carrying trays of plastic cups. When she was near enough, she called out to Jessica.

"Hi, Jess! Can you get me a drink? Mum and Dad say they won't bother, they're too busy chatting. I've got some money here." Jessica nodded; it was too noisy to reply. Holly watched as she carefully edged her way back through the queue.

"Phew! Made it!" Jessica handed a cup of orange squash to Holly. "Let's sit on the steps outside; it's getting really hot in here."

It was still daylight as they pushed open the doors on to the street. The rain had stopped, and the sky was clearing. "Your sister's in the next half, isn't she?" Jessica asked. "Bet she's nervous. Hey, didn't I see you at the museum this morning? You were deep in conversation with a bloke in a tweed suit."

"That's Mr. Edwards. He's the curator. He's, er, well, he's sort of helping me with my project. I didn't see you. Where were you?" Holly, irrationally, felt slightly annoyed.

"In the room with the French kids. I was actually only walking through. Hang on, we haven't got a project! We haven't, have we? Am I supposed to be doing something? Mum'd kill me if I forgot to do holiday work." Jessica looked worried.

"Oh no, it's okay It's just something I wanted to do. You don't have to do it." She drank her orange squash and stood up. "Don't you think we'd better get back? The second half'll be starting any minute." Holly was keen to change the subject. Maybe one day she'd tell Jessica about her adventures, but not now, not yet.

Miss Rider herself came through the gap in the closed curtains to introduce the second half. There was immediate applause and some stamping of feet from the back.

"Ladies and gentleman, boys and girls," she smiled broadly, blushing slightly. "For our second half, we have strayed a little from our traditional pattern of ballet and mime. The older girls were keen to try something new and so, as many of you know, I started a class of modern dance last term. My girls have worked hard and have produced something of which—" she gave a little cough and blushed again, "'Top of the Pops' would be proud." More applause. "Thank you, thank you very much. So, welcome to our Magic Toy Shop!"

She stepped back behind the curtains which then gradually drew apart. Soft blue light shone on the silent scene. Girls dressed as clowns, Barbie dolls, and Telly Tubbies stood quite still. Leaning stiffly against the shop counter at the back was a girl in a sparkly black leotard, gold tights, and a long blonde wig. It was Beth, the Pop Idol doll.

All was quiet except for a few coughs from the audience and, once again, a feeling of expectancy hung in the air. Then, with a single twang of an acoustic guitar, the disco lights started. The music, soft at first, rose to a crescendo and the Toy Shop came to life.

The Telly Tubbies were first, bobbing and swaying, followed by the clowns and the Barbie dolls, all in step to the 1960s' Cliff Richard song, 'Living Doll.' The audience loved it; some began clapping in rhythm.

The music died away and then rose again. To the strains of Kylie Minogue's 'I Can't Get You Out of My Head,' Beth, the Pop Idol doll, straightened up, bowed low, and sprang to the front of the stage.

Her dancing was brilliant, fast, and exciting. Even Holly had to admit it. The disco lights threw every colour of the rainbow from their mirrored facets onto the vibrant scene so that Beth seemed to be dancing with the light, catching it, throwing it, leaping over it. The little children on the cushions at the front started jumping up and down in time to the music. Some teenagers at the back started a Mexican wave.

When the show ended, there was uproar. People sprang to their feet to clap. There were shouts of "Encore! Encore!" When Miss Rider appeared in the spotlight blushing pinker than ever, someone started singing "For she's a jolly good fellow!"

Miss Rider beamed. If this were the last show she ever did, she'd rest happy.

For the finale, all the dancers, littlest first, came to take a bow. At the end, Emily ran to the back of the stage and came forward with a bouquet of flowers almost as big as herself to present to her adored teacher.

Miss Rider held up her hand for silence.

"Thank you, dear lovely people. Your children are stars. They are all stars." More applause. "Between us all, we have managed to raise more money to help restore this fine old hall to its former—or future—" Miss Rider smiled at the ripple of laughter, "glory. Thanks to our generous sponsor, the Hawkes-Lewis Endowment Fund..."

Holly started. What name did she say? Did she imagine it? She'd

heard that name before. It was at the museum, on their first visit. "…
we have no expenses and every penny will go to help restore this
hall." Even more applause.

Soon, the audience was streaming out through the double doors,
excited, tired children in tow. Beth was greeted by hugs and praise
from everyone, especially her family. She felt ecstatic.

"It's been the best night in my whole, whole life!" she announced
as Stephen and Katy almost carried her to the car.

The moon had risen, huge and silver above the rooftops, and the
evening star twinkled in the deep blue sky. As they squeezed into the
car, Holly grabbed the programme.

"Beth, you've got to sign it. It'll be special then. It might be worth
a lot of money when you're a prima ballerina."

"Or a Pop Idol," added Stephen.

Taking a pen from the glove box, Holly passed it to her exhausted
sister.

"By the way," said Katy from the front passenger seat, "who was it
Miss Rider said sponsored the show? I don't remember there being a
sponsor before."

Holly had to be sure. She turned to the back page of the pro-
gramme. There it was, in small print right at the bottom. She read out:
"This performance is sponsored by the Hawkes-Lewis Endowment
Fund."

9

Beth fell asleep as soon as her head touched the pillow, her mug of hot chocolate left untouched on the bedside table. But Holly's brain would not let her sleep. The happenings of the last few days were crowding into her mind, becoming tangled up, confusing the past with the present.

On the edge of sleep, she imagined herself on the platform of the railway station which Mr. Edwards had described. Marjorie was with her in her fairy costume, dancing through the crowds with Peter running along at her heels. Then the station became the beach hut and the painter was there with his box of numbers, offering Holly a deck chair to sit in. Someone was saying, "We'll fetch Mrs. Hawkes-Lewis, she'll know what to do," when Holly managed to pull herself back to the present.

She sat up, put on the bedside table lamp, and reached for a pencil and paper. There were the trails again, leading her somewhere, providing clues. If she wrote them down, it would help her to sleep, she was sure.

So she wrote: Who is Mrs. Hawkes-Lewis? Does she/did she know Marjorie? Thinks: Yes. Why? Don't know. Feels right.

Clues: 1) Very old lady. 2) Museum, she gave the bells. 3) She lived in St. Aubyn's all her life. 4) Best clue: Her name was Mia. Mia's short for Amelia. The girl with red hair was called Amelia. 5) Dancing…

Holly's pencil fell from her hand, the pad of paper slid to the floor, and she was fast asleep.

§ § § § § §

The next morning, Beth was up first, full of fun and determined that everyone else should be too. She knocked loudly on her parents' bedroom door.

"Come on, Mummy and Daddy! You'll be late for church. You've got to get up now or you won't have time for breakfast."

This was Katy's weekly plea to her younger daughter as she pulled back the duvet from her sleepy head.

No answer, just deep snores from Stephen.

Beth knocked again, more loudly this time. "I'll be first in the bathroom then! I may be a long time. I've got to wash my hair. Don't you want to get in first?"

"'Morning, princess," called out Stephen, yawning. "You must have slept well. Hang on, it's only eight o'clock. Time for another quick snooze."

Some very phoney, very loud snoring was heard from behind the bedroom door, along with muffled laughter from Katy.

"Parents! What can you do with them?" said Beth, with a very exaggerated sigh, and went to attack Holly's door. It was wide open, but the bathroom door was shut. Beth could hear the shower running.

"I might be a long time!" called out Holly. "Just washing my hair."

§ § § § § §

The church congregation that morning was swelled by a number of holidaymakers and a visiting choir who were to sing the anthem and perform a short canticle after the service. The Vicar, Rev. Clive Brown, was on holiday, and a rather elderly clergyman had been called in to take his place. He had wispy white hair and was very short with a round, slightly pink, face. He was Rev. Robin Littlejohn, a name which splendidly matched his appearance.

He knew none of the music for the responses and sang dreadfully out of tune, to the amusement of both the girls.

Katy whispered, "We've got to sing loudly, then maybe he'll follow us." It didn't work.

The next problem he had was with the list of names to be read out in the prayers for the sick. There was quite a long list, and he read it very slowly, pronouncing every syllable.

"Miss Van-ess-a Bur-ber-ry; Mrs. An-gel-a Foth-er-ing-ton..." he intoned.

Holly nudged Beth and whispered, "We'll be here all day at this rate. I wish I'd brought some sandwiches." Beth giggled.

The voice went on: "Mr. Jim Gar-den-er and (cough) Mrs. Mi-a Hawkes-Lew-is…"

Holly dropped her prayer book on the floor. There was that name again! It was a name she'd never heard until this holiday, and now she'd heard it three times. It just had to mean something.

§ § § § § §

Because of the choir's performance after the service, they arrived home later than usual. Katy hurried to get the lunch ready, issuing jobs to both the girls and Stephen.

"Mummy, we've got to visit Mrs. Hawkes-Lewis. We must go this afternoon. Please!"

Holly was sitting at the kitchen table shelling peas. Beth had gone into the garden with Stephen to pick raspberries for pudding.

"It was strange her name should be read out when we heard it only last night," said Katy, "but why do you want to see her? We don't even know her." She put the potatoes in the saucepan to par-boil before placing them in the oven with the chicken.

"Yes, but we do sort of know her," said Holly. "She sponsored the show, at least her name did. And Mr. Edwards mentioned her when we went to the museum a couple of weeks ago. She gave the bells that were in the room where we saw the waxwork models of the little girl and the lady."

"But why today?" said Katy, retrieving a potato from the floor. She washed it and put it in the pan with the others. "Anyway, she's proba-bly in hospital."

"Then we must find out. We know she lives in Rottingdean and Hawkes-Lewis is a pretty unusual name. She's probably in the phone book," Holly said as she popped a particularly large peapod over the colander.

"But why today?" Katy repeated. "People like to keep Sundays for their families, and anyway—"

"Don't you *see?* She might die! She's really old, and now she's ill. She could die any minute. I'm absolutely positive she knows the friends I met in 1914 and—"

"Oh, Holly, I really don't think I can go through all that again. I do want to believe you, but I honestly can't take it in. I'm not saying you're lying or anything, but—"

"But what? Look, if you come and meet Mrs. Hawkes-Lewis, and she *was* there in 1914 and met me, then you'd be convinced, wouldn't you? Okay, I know she's really old and for her it was a long time ago, but sometimes when people are very old they remember things ages ago very clearly. Mrs. Howard told us that once. And anyway, apart from that, Mr. Edwards said she had a story about the bells she wanted to tell him. She could tell us, and we'll pass it on." Holly handed the colander of shelled peas to her mother. "And you'd never guess, Mummy, but Mr. Edwards has…"

"Tell us what?" said Stephen as he and Beth came into the kitchen with two large bowls of raspberries. Holly had missed her chance. Mr. Edwards's story would remain untold.

"Oh, Holly says she wants to go and see Mrs. Hawkes-Lewis, the lady we prayed for in church this morning. Her name was on the programme last night, you remember? I told her I didn't think Sunday was a good day."

"Well, I've got to get back to work this afternoon, I'm afraid. One of the staff is off sick, and if we're going to try to get away on holiday on Friday, I need to make sure the Garden Centre keeps running smoothly. Sunday afternoon's a busy time." Stephen put down the raspberries and began to lay the table. "Sorry about that."

§ § § § §

The afternoon was bright and sunny, but with a cold wind, too cold for the beach, and by the time they got out, it was already after four o'clock. Holly had found the name Hawkes-Lewis in the phone book, and with Beth's help had managed to persuade Katy they should visit. They'd tried to phone, but there was no reply. Katy had serious misgivings, but she could tell her daughters would not be happy until they had at least tried to see the old lady.

They drove along the coast road towards Rottingdean, high up above the cliffs with the blue sea sparkling in the distance. Holly's excitement was mounting. Would she solve the mystery this very afternoon? Would she at least find out who Marjorie is and why they'd met? Beth seemed to catch her mood, but as they drew nearer, doubts began to creep into Holly's mind. Suppose Mrs. Hawkes-Lewis wasn't in? After all, no one had answered the phone. Or suppose she was in, but too ill to see them? Suppose she remembered nothing at all of her childhood? Or, worst of all, suppose she had died?

The address they were looking for was 11, Bellevue Road East. Katy's Brighton street map didn't go this far, so they would have to ask the way if they didn't spot the road. But then Beth called out: "Look! There's Bellevue Road West. Over there, by that pub."

"Well spotted, Beth," said Katy, slowing down. "Bellevue Road East must go the other way at that crossroads."

She carefully turned the car round and changed gear to drive up the steep hill.

They found the house easily. It was a pretty, white-painted bungalow, and its yellow front door had a round stained glass window at the top with the design of a sunset. Two small box trees stood in tubs at either side of the front door and a hanging basket filled with petunias and blue lobelia, freshly watered, partly obscured the lace-curtained window behind it.

Holly's heart began to beat fast as Katy grasped the polished brass knocker in the shape of a fish, its tail uppermost. They couldn't see a bell. She knocked twice, but there was no answer.

"Someone must be in," said Holly. "Those flowers have just been watered. Look, they're dripping."

She turned to peer through the bay window on the left. She could see a sofa bed with floral cushions carefully arranged up one end and a pink blanket, neatly folded. On a little mahogany table next to the sofa bed a book lay open beside a half-full glass of water. But there was no one there.

"Don't stare through the window, Holly, it's rude! And anyway, the old lady might be there and you'd give her a dreadful shock," said Katy. "I'll try knocking once more, but if there's still no answer, we'll have to go."

Feeling rather as if she were intruding, Katy grasped the bronze fish knocker again and brought it down sharply twice more.

Still silence. No curtain moved, no footsteps could be heard. Beth pushed open the letterbox and tried to peep in, but there was some kind of container the other side for catching letters and she could see nothing.

"Come on, this is silly." Katy turned to walk back up the path. "We can't go looking through letterboxes and staring through windows of a complete stranger. Obviously no one's in; we'll just have to try another day. Come on now." She had her hand on the little wrought iron gate when Beth called out, "No, wait! I can hear something. It's coming from the garden."

"It's a mower!" cried Holly. "Someone's mowing the lawn. Look, there's a side gate over there. I'm going in." She ran round the front of the bungalow and disappeared out of sight.

Katy wasn't quick enough to stop her. She felt uncomfortable about Holly's actions and was already mentally apologising to whoever was in the garden. But she and Beth followed Holly through the gate.

A tall, slim man of about fifty years old, shirtsleeves rolled up, was down the far end of the garden, skillfully creating broad green stripes on the smooth lawn with a large electric mower. The orange flex trailed across the garden, round an ornamental pond, and through the kitchen window, presumably to a power point inside.

He must have spotted Holly because he turned off the mower.

"Hello, can I help you?" he called out as he walked towards her. "Have you been knocking? I'm sorry, I can't hear a thing down here."

He seemed friendly enough. Katy hurried over to him. "I'm so sorry. Yes, we did knock, but my daughter should not have just walked into your garden like this. I really don't know what to say."

"Oh, that's all right," said the man. "I've got daughters myself, though they're a bit older than you two." He smiled at Holly and Beth. "They're eighteen—both of them, twins, you see—but I well remember what they were like at your age. Were you looking for me?" He addressed Holly this time.

"Well actually, we've...er...we've come to see if Mrs. Hawkes-Lewis is okay. The Vicar gave out her name in church this morning with the people who are ill." Holly looked a bit embarrassed.

"Yes, and her name was on the programme at my dancing show last night," added Beth.

The man nodded. "The School of Dancing. Of course." He looked thoughtful. "That was nice of the Vicar; she'd been poorly for a while, just old age really. Look, you'd better come inside."

They followed him into the kitchen. The draining board was piled high with clean dishes, and a number of saucepans were stacked inside each other on the blue Formica table. An enormous bunch of pink and yellow roses was soaking in a bucket on the floor. Several tea towels had been hung up to dry on a small line above the boiler. Holly noticed one had a design of Brighton Pavilion on it and another was from Majorca.

"Please excuse all this untidiness," he said as he showed them through to the hall where they could see the round stained glass window from the other side. "The family left in a bit of a hurry. Come on into the lounge."

He started to show them into the room Holly had seen through the bay window but then he stopped and said, "On second thoughts, I think the conservatory would be better. Please, do come this way."

The conservatory was sunny and cheerful. Cane furniture with orange padded cushions almost filled what space was left by the large collection of beautiful potted ferns and flowers that stood on the black and white tiled floor. Their host indicated that Katy and the girls should sit down.

Katy was feeling increasingly uncomfortable. Something was amiss here. She plucked up courage and asked, "How is Mrs. Hawkes-Lewis? We do hope she's feeling better."

Both the girls nodded. Beth shifted on her cushion nervously and seemed to be taking an unnatural interest in the plants, stroking the leaves of the fern nearest to her.

Holly knew what was coming, and she could hardly bear it.

"I'm so sorry, but my grandmother died early this afternoon."

10

Holly didn't mean to say it; she just couldn't help herself.

"Oh no! She can't have, she just can't have! I really, really wanted to see her." She was near to tears.

Katy grabbed her hand and held it tightly. "I'm so very, very sorry," she apologised. "Please forgive us for intruding at such a sad time. Look, we'll go immediately." She got up, taking Beth's hand as well.

"No, please don't go," said Mrs. Hawkes-Lewis's grandson, "I can assure you, it wasn't sad at all, only insofar as she isn't with us anymore. Look, let me make you a cup of tea, and I'll tell you about it. No, really…"

Katy tried to protest.

"I love to talk about Gran. I won't be a minute."

Katy and the girls sat there in silence while he went to the kitchen. Holly looked devastated. Beth went on stroking the fern.

He returned carrying a polished wooden tray with wicker handles laden with a teapot in a striped woolly tea cosy with a bobble on the top, four willow pattern cups and saucers, and a matching milk jug.

"Oh, I forgot to ask you. Would you girls prefer squash? I know Gran had some."

They assured him tea was fine.

"Now," he said, "first of all, may I ask your names? I'm Roland Hawkes-Lewis." He carefully poured the tea as they introduced themselves in turn.

"Did you know my grandmother well?" he asked. "She's been a bit of a recluse the last few years, but we took her out as often as we could. Holly, you said you needed to see her. How did you come to know her?"

Holly, to the amazement of her mother, didn't hesitate: "I think I met her when she was younger. A lot younger."

Roland Hawkes-Lewis laughed. "You're not old enough! But you tell me anyway. Where did you meet her?"

"On the beach." She was Amelia, Holly was sure, the girl with the crinkly ginger hair. "She was on the beach, and there were lots of other children there. It wasn't for very long, but, well, I just remember her. I was so hoping she'd remember me."

Roland looked puzzled. "It's a long time since we got her to the beach; you must have been very young. Are you sure it was my grandmother?"

"Yes, I'm really sure." Holly was on the verge of adding, "It was only on Friday," but managed to stop herself just in time.

Beth suddenly said, "Did your granny die here? Why aren't you sad?"

Katy was horrified. "Beth, you mustn't say that! Mr. Hawkes-Lewis, I'm so sorry."

"No, no. Don't be. And do call me Roland. I'll tell you, Beth, why I'm not sad. It was Gran's one hundred and first birthday. We were all here, my wife, Susan, and our daughters, Lizzy and Jo. We had an early lunch because the girls were leaving for Gatwick this afternoon. The holiday to Crete was their eighteenth birthday present from their great-grandma. Gran was so happy. Although she really wasn't well enough, at her insistence we'd had a big party for her last Saturday with all the family, but she wanted to see the girls again before they left.

"Then she said a strange thing. We thought her mind was wandering; it happened quite often recently. We'd just finished lunch when she suddenly said, 'Do you know, I think it's time I left now. I'm quite ready for the journey.' We thought she was confused, that she meant Lizzy and Jo. But not Gran. She knew what she was saying."

"Did she die then?" asked Beth, to Katy's dismay. But Roland was unperturbed.

"No, not then. She said goodbye to the girls and told them to think of her when they were in Crete. Then they left with Susan to drive to Gatwick. Gran turned to me and said, 'So, all's well. Will you mow the lawn after I've gone? I'd like a sleep now.' I helped her on to the sofa bed and she just fell asleep, smiling. She died in her sleep. How could I be sad? It was just as she wanted it to be, and she was so happy. And now you know why I was mowing the lawn this afternoon."

Sensing his guests were at a loss as to what to say, Roland quickly changed the subject. "Now, Beth. Tell me about the show. Gran so much wanted to be there."

When Beth had finished her vivid description of the show, which Roland seemed genuinely to enjoy, he said, "Do you know, Gran was actually convinced she was there. At the show, I mean. She told us she'd gone to watch her friend who loved to dance."

A shiver ran down Holly's spine. A friend who loved to dance? It had to be Marjorie.

"Yes, she wanted the Hawkes-Lewis Trust income to support the dancing school. You saw the name Hawkes-Lewis on the programme, you said? Well, the endowment fund was started by her mother-in-law in memory of my great uncle. He lost his sight at the Battle of the Somme in the First World War. He never really recovered from his injuries and died in 1920."

Holly's mind was racing. Maybe it was racing too fast; she so much wanted to believe that Roland's grandmother was Amelia. Then she suddenly remembered Dulcie's words as they huddled together in the tent on the beach: "Josh has got a pash on Amelia." He must have married her! Josh's name had to be Hawkes-Lewis. So his brother did go to war, and he was blinded and then he died. It was too much, too much for her to take in. It was only the day before yesterday when they'd talked on the beach and Josh, full of courage and excitement, had said he wanted to go and fight the Kaiser. But his brother died, blinded probably from gas in some ghastly trench in a murderous battle.

Roland was still talking. "For many years, the trust income went to St. Dunstan's and other local charities that helped the blind. My great-grandparents died in the 1930s, and my grandfather died in 1942. He was a fighter pilot, you know; he was shot down over France. So Gran was the sole remaining trustee. She chose many different causes to support in recent years."

What was he talking about? Why was he talking about trusts and things she didn't understand? Holly began to think about her time on the beach only two days ago. The room was warm and her eyelids were becoming heavy. She imagined she was sitting in the tent on the beach with Marjorie and Dulcie and Josh, and there was Amelia looking in, with her gold-grey eyes and her crinkly ginger hair, young and bright and happy. How could she be a very old lady who had just died? Could she, Holly, be losing her mind?

But now Roland was saying something important.

"This year she was determined that it should be Miss Anne Rider's School of Dancing. She insisted it was for her friend who loved dancing."

Holly was suddenly alert again. "She didn't tell you the friend's name, did she?" She hardly dared to ask.

"No. No, I'm afraid not. But she said..." he looked at Holly strangely. "She said they played on the beach together. Gran was the only girl in her family; she had five brothers, three of them older than her, and it seems that she sort of adopted this little girl as a younger sister. She was very fond of her."

Holly nodded. "And did she ever tell you anything about the bells? The bells in the museum, the ones she gave?"

"You know about those? Well, my father took them down for her from her old house in St. Aubyn's. They've turned the house into flats now like all the others. But no, I'm afraid she never told us the story about them. I think she always meant to, but sadly it has died with her."

§ § § § §

As they drove away from 11, Bellevue Road East, Katy didn't turn back towards Brighton; she headed for the Downs.

"I think after all this emotion we need to get out and stretch our legs and feel the wind in our hair. How about it?" She was determined to break the atmosphere of gloom that had descended on both the girls.

"Okay," was all Holly said.

"It was a bit spooky, wasn't it?" said Beth. "I mean, there we were in that house where someone had just *died*. I bet that's why he took us into the conservatory, because the old lady had died in the other room. It's spooky, isn't it?"

"No, it's not!" said Holly. "She was happy. Roland said so. I just wish so much that, oh, I don't know." She lapsed into silence. Beth looked annoyed.

"I think we'll head for Ditchling Beacon," said Katy. "It won't take long, and it will be lovely up there."

Although it was late in the afternoon, the sun was still high. The blueness of the sky was broken only by little, white, scudding clouds that cast racing shadows on the smooth green turf. They could see for miles. The curve of the Downs stretched away in both directions, the sea a silver strip in the far distance.

They ran along the ridge of the Downs, Beth holding her arms out like an aeroplane. Holly's mood began to lift, and in a few moments, she too was running with arms outstretched, feeling the wind in her long hair and the late afternoon sun on her face. *Yes,* she thought, *it will be all right. One of my trails might have come to a dead end, but it will be all right. When one door closes, another opens.* It was a favourite saying of her grandmother's.

Stephen was just back from the Garden Centre when they arrived home. He looked exhausted.

"I really don't know how I'm going to cope with all the work," he said over supper. "Katy, love, do you think there's any chance you could come and help out with the paperwork? I'm getting way behind with the accounts. Perhaps the girls could go to a friend's?"

"Well, Holly, you've got Science Club in the morning, haven't you? And Beth, you've got crafts. Maybe you could go to Jessica's for lunch? I could give you the key to the beach hut for later on; Jessica's mother was asking the other day if they could use it some time. I'll give her a ring. Daddy really needs my help if we're ever going to get away on holiday."

§ § § § §

Before they went to bed that night, Holly grabbed Beth's arm and pulled her into her bedroom. She looked along the empty landing then shut the door carefully behind her and drew the long, yellow curtains across the big sash windows.

"Right," she said. "We need a plan of action. Time's running out; we've only got a few days left to solve the mystery before we go away. We've got to find out why we could go back to 1914 and, most especially, who Marjorie is. Mr. Edwards said we were 'there by grace.' I'm still not really sure what he meant, but I think it's sort of special to us, like a gift. There's so much I want to know, we've got to go back there."

"Did you tell Mr. Edwards?" Beth was horrified. "That's stupid! He must think you're mad. What else did he say?"

"Lots and lots. I can't tell you all about it now because it's late but actually it happened to him, too. He said no one believed him. Not ever. Not until now, that is, when he told me. Hang on," Holly opened the door a crack. "Mummy's coming." She closed the door quietly.

"I've tried to tell her about everything, but she doesn't really believe me, so I can't try to explain now. We've just got to try to get back there tomorrow."

"You mean we try when we're with Jess?" Beth sat down on the bed and wrapped Holly's sunflower patterned duvet round her. It was chilly now. "It didn't happen when I was with Alice in the beach hut." She sounded doubtful. "We had the doors shut and everything, but nothing happened."

"I know, but we've got to try. It may already be too late. Marjorie said when I went on my own that they were going home at the week-end, but her time and ours aren't the same. We'd moved on about three weeks, but in 1914 it was only a few days later. There's no way of telling. "

"But maybe this time it will be the same day, and they'll all have gone and no one will know us and it will be scary. We might even end up in a different time altogether. Maybe we'd better not try." Beth looked worried. She was still just a little afraid.

"No, no, that wouldn't happen. We're there because of Marjorie, I'm positive. Anyway, she asked me to be sure to bring you next time. I said I would, so you've got to come. Don't think too much now or you won't get to sleep, but I'm telling you, it will be a brilliant adventure."

11

Monday morning began much the same as any other day. The houses looked the same as they always did, many with long net curtains at the windows, which, unless you peered closely, kept hidden the rooms and people within. But this morning, some of the sashes had been flung up to let in the sunshine as if to say "Welcome! Come on in, there are no secrets here."

Most of the houses in the road where the Randall family lived had been built around the beginning of the last century, red brick and gabled with tall sash windows and wide stone sills. A few had been divided into flats, and inside the front archways were rows of buttons for entry phones with a small white card against each one announcing the number and the occupier's name: 1.Smith 2.Clarkson and so on. They reminded Holly of exam results, the poor Newnhams in the largest flat always coming bottom at number seven.

Children played in the front garden of the house on the corner, kicking a football on the worn-out grass, falling over each other and laughing as a small puppy joined in the fun.

Old Mrs. Dixon from the other side of the road gave Holly and Beth a wave as she manoeuvred her shopping basket on wheels carefully out of her front gate, a green patterned headscarf tied neatly under her chin to protect her new permanent wave from the morning breeze.

It seemed an ordinary day.

A dark blue estate car pulled up as the girls reached the top of the road. It was Jenny, Jessica's mother.

"Hi, girls!" Jenny greeted them as they climbed in. "How are you this morning? It looks as if it's going to be a really hot day, I thought we might take a picnic down to your beach hut later, if that's all right?"

"That'd be great," said Holly, "Mum gave me the key."

They dropped Beth off first for Craft Club. "Have fun, Beth. Bring us back a pot or a nice bowl," said Jenny as she opened the door for her.

"It's collage this morning," said Beth. "Oh no, I've forgotten my magazine cuttings! I had them all out ready to bring. Mummy was going to remind me. Can we go back? I've got have something to cut out."

"I expect Mummy was in a bit of a rush to get off to the Garden Centre. Here," said Jenny, reaching down onto the floor of the front passenger seat, "will this do? It's yesterday's Sunday Telegraph magazine, and there're some lovely fashion photos in it. Oh, and something on African wildlife. See you back here at about twelve o'clock?"

"Okay. Thanks." Beth ran off, happily clutching the magazine.

Jenny drove on to take Jessica and Holly to their school for Science Club. "Have a good morning," she said. "Don't blow up the school, will you?"

Jessica sighed; she'd heard her mother's joke too many times before.

§ § § § §

It always seemed strange being at school during the holidays. Apart from the science lab, everywhere was so unnaturally quiet, no shouts and laughter from the playground, no bells to summon you in to lessons. "Like a ghost school," Jessica had once said.

The subject for this morning was comets. Mrs. Howard asked those who had seen it to describe in turn their impression of the wonderful, bright light which had been the comet Hale Bopp. There had to be little or no light pollution, she had told them, to be able to see it properly, but if you had been lucky enough to be in such a place, you would never forget it. How did it make them feel?

Holly had seen it. Mum and Dad had taken them up onto the Downs to watch, she told the class. It had appeared like a huge headlight out of the dark sky, its long tail stretched across the heavens, unreal, like the visitor from outer space that it was. She would certainly never forget it.

It was a lively discussion, but Holly had been so hoping they would go on studying the theme of time and space. She was trying to think of some way to bring the subject up again when, just before mid-morning break, Mrs. Howard said, "Isn't the world wonderful? We are so privileged to have seen this amazing phenomenon, crossing time and space."

This was Holly's cue. She had just fifteen minutes before the second session to talk to Mrs. Howard on her own. She waited until all the other girls had left the room. Luckily, Jess was deep in conversation with another girl and didn't notice that Holly had remained behind.

"Mrs. Howard, can I ask you something? It's really important." Holly pulled up a chair to sit beside the teacher at her desk.

"Fire away. Have a Mars Bar."

Holly took it and began to slowly unwrap the paper.

"You know what you were saying the other day about being able to see back into the past across light years if there was a telescope clever enough?"

"Sadly, it's not been invented yet. Wouldn't it be just wonderful if we could?" Mrs. Howard took a bite of her Mars Bar.

"Yes, but seriously, if all time exists at once, so to speak, do you think we could ever actually sort of slip into the past? Or the future, come to that? I mean could it just sort of happen without anything happening to make it happen, if you see what I mean?"

"How I'd love to believe it could!" said Mrs. Howard. "Mind you, there are some periods of history I would definitely choose to miss. The Black Death in 1349 would be one of them, and 1665 and the Great Plague followed by the fire. But think of being around at the time of the Great Discoverers—all that uncharted territory! But you'd have to be sure to be able to get back to your own time again, of course. Enough of that; I must think carefully about your question."

She poured herself a cup of lemonade and offered one to Holly.

"There is a theory," she continued, "that time runs in parallel: the past, present, and future side by side. If this theory is correct, then maybe there are times when we can cross over from one parallel to another. I think it's easier when you're young. Your mind gets so crowded as you get older that it blots out things that don't seem to have a rational explanation as being simply fanciful or downright untrue. We should remember that we don't always see things as they really are. As I was talking about parallels, we'll take that as an example. We know, for instance, that a motorway of a certain width will run, with slight variations, for as long as it goes with that same width. But if we were to look down a long straight stretch of the motorway, it would appear that the lines of the road gradually run together to a point at which they disappear. Are you with me?"

"Yes, I think so," said Holly. "I know what you mean. We talked about that in art class when we were studying perspective."

"Now that's a very good example," said Mrs. Howard. "You've got the idea, then? I expect you were told that the point at which the lines disappear altogether is called the vanishing point. Perhaps this can happen with parallels of time. Could time have a vanishing point? I don't know. As I'm a scientist, it may sound strange to say I firmly believe that we are not meant to know everything. You hear people say that there's always got to be a rational explanation for this or that. But there hasn't. The world would be an awfully dull place if we could explain everything away, and absolutely no challenge for us scientists. There'd be no mysteries." She paused to finish her Mars Bar and replace her spectacles, which she'd balanced like a hair band on top of her straight grey hair. "So," Mrs. Howard continued, "if we are fortunate enough to find ourselves in some exciting situation which seems like a miracle, or see something in some way which others don't but which enriches our lives, then that is a gift from God, and we should be thankful for it."

"I think I see what you mean. You don't think it matters that we don't understand?" Holly finished her Mars Bar and threw the wrapper into the waste paper basket.

"No. We have to take some things by faith, on trust. That's not to say, of course, that we scientists—and that includes you, Holly—shouldn't continue searching."

"There's just something else I wanted to ask you about..." Holly began when the door of the lab opened and the other girls began to come back into the room. Break time, it seemed, had ended.

"Maybe some other time," said Mrs. Howard. "Remind me next term."

At the end of the second session, Mrs. Howard stood up and leaned forward on her desk.

"Thank you all for coming this morning and for all your contributions. I'm off to catch a train up to London now to a lecture on the effect of the moon's pull on the earth's surface. It's not just water that's affected, you know. There are still new theories and new evidence. Should be fascinating. I'll tell you about it next term. Enjoy the rest of the holidays!"

As she was locking the lab door, Mrs. Howard said quietly to Holly, who had come to say goodbye, "I enjoyed our little chat; it's got me thinking. Keep an open mind and don't reject miracles. Oh, and have fun!"

It was the last session of Science Club for the summer.

§§§§§

Mr. Jim, who kept a watchful eye on all the beach huts, had a grandson of whom he was inordinately proud. Young Jim, as his grandfather called him, although everyone else knew him as Jamie, was a lifeguard on Brighton beach when he wasn't studying Information Technology at Sussex University. On this hot afternoon, he was sitting on the prow of the rescue boat, a bikini-clad girl on either side of him. One, who looked remarkably like a Barbie doll, had her arm draped around his bronzed neck.

"Get off!" said Jamie, disengaging himself from her embrace, "Can't you see I'm on duty? I can't be doing with this now."

The girl flung back her mane of yellow hair and tried to hold his hand instead. Jamie got up, pushing her away just as Holly, Beth and Jessica, followed a few yards behind by Jenny, were making their way through the crowds to the sea's edge.

"Hiya, girls!" he said, "How y'doing? Not got the boat with you today?"

"Jessica's mum thought it would be too crowded in the water," said Holly. "We're just going to have a quick swim before lunch 'cos we're starving."

"Well done, Jessica's mum. You'll be one less to rescue. I've already had to pull in a little kiddie in a Big Tyre rubber ring. Floating way out, he was, and he couldn't have been more than four years old. Stupid mother didn't even realise he'd gone out in it, just lay sunning herself with her headphones on without a care in the world."

"You were wonderful, Jamie!" The Barbie doll who had doggedly stayed at his side took his hand again. "So brave. That little boy could've drowned."

"Get off!" said Jamie, more firmly this time. "Yes, he could have, but it wasn't brave, it's what I'm here for. Anyway, girls, don't go out too far, and watch out for windsurfers. They're banned from this beach, but that doesn't stop them." Pushing Barbie away again, he returned to his seat on the boat.

The sea was gloriously warm. They managed to make their way through the small children and non-swimmers at the water's edge and

head out into deeper water. They were all strong swimmers. Beth
floated on her back kicking spray into the air, the droplets of water
sparkling as they caught the sun's rays. Away from the crowds, they
could swim freely, ducking underwater and picking up stones from
the seabed.

After a little while Jenny said, "I think we'd better get back now. I
don't know about you, but I'm really hungry. We can have another
swim later on."

As they reached the shore, Jessica let out a scream.

"Oh, my foot! I've trodden on something. Owwww!" She sat down
on the wet stones and looked at her foot. It was bleeding profusely.
"It's glass," she said, "I've trodden on some glass—it's agony, I can't
move." The colour had drained from her face.

"Oh, you poor thing!" said Holly, putting her arm round Jessica's
shoulders. "Look, Jamie's coming; he'll know what to do."

Jenny rushed to her daughter's side just as Jamie, hearing the
shout, arrived on the scene. Jenny held up a jagged piece of glass
from a broken beer bottle.

"That's what did it!" she said, as she tried to comfort Jessica who
was sobbing. "How could anyone be so stupid as to leave a broken
bottle on the beach with all these children about?"

A small crowd had gathered. Someone offered a clean handkerchief which Jenny gratefully accepted.

"Move back, please, and give the girl some air." Jamie quickly took
control. "We'll soon have you right as rain, Jess. Mum, put your
hands tightly round her foot—yes, just like that—and keep them
there. Back in a sec."

He sprinted up the beach, jumping deftly over sunbathers and picnic baskets to the rescue boat and the first aid box, returning with a
thick pad of lint, a crepe bandage, a big towel, and a can of Coca-
Cola. Jenny's hands were beginning to ache, but she'd stemmed the
flow of blood.

"Right," said Jamie, "You okay, Jess?" She shook her head; she
was shivering. Jamie wrapped the towel firmly round her and held the
pad of lint ready.

"Now, Mum, you can let go." As soon as Jenny removed the hankie
from her daughter's foot, Jamie slapped the pad onto the wound.

"Can you hold that in place for me?" he asked Jessica. The hand-
some lifeguard's attention seemed to be having a therapeutic effect on
his patient and her colour began to return. Jamie opened the can of

Coca-Cola and handed it to her. "Drink this, just a sip at a time; it'll make you feel better. You've had quite a shock."

She took a sip of the cola and then held her hands over the pad. She even managed a little smile. In a matter of seconds, Jamie had the bandage fastened expertly round her foot.

"One thing," he said, "with all that bleeding, you've probably washed out any small shards of glass from the wound. But you might need stitches. There's a St. John's Ambulance station a couple of hundred yards down the prom towards the West Pier. Do you think you can make it, or shall I carry you?"

"Well, you might just have to," sighed Jess, to the fury of Barbie who was sulking nearby. "I don't think I can stand."

"Oh, I think we could give it a try," said Jenny. "Jamie might be needed in another emergency. Look, your flip-flops are here, and now you're bandaged and warm, I think we'll be able to make it together. Thank you so much, Jamie."

"Think nothing of it, ma'am," Jamie affected a pseudo American accent. "All part o' the service." Then, reverting to his local accent, he added, "But if I get my hands on the loser who left that broken bottle there, I'll kill 'im!"

Between them, Holly and Jenny helped Jess up the beach to the prom. She gingerly put her foot to the ground and winced but managed to walk a few steps.

"I'll stay here," said Beth, sitting on the wall opposite the beach hut. "I might have to eat some sandwiches." Realising this sounded a bit heartless, she quickly added, "I'm really sorry about your foot, Jess."

"Of course you can have some sandwiches," said Jenny. "But look, Holly, we'll be okay now, won't we, Jess? You stay with Beth. You won't go in the sea again now, will you?" Holly assured her they were far too hungry. "We'll see you in a few minutes, then. I'll come back and tell you what's happening if we're going to be any length of time."

Holly untied the beach hut key from the strap of her swimsuit where she always kept it when they were swimming. She began to open the padlock when Beth said, "Oh no! I left my flip-flops on the beach. Won't be a minute." And she was off down the steps, running over the stones through the crowds, something Holly could never do in bare feet.

The bright pink flip-flops were where she'd left them, next to the rescue boat. Jamie was still sitting on the prow, but this time with two different girls. He spotted Beth as she slipped her feet into the flip-flops.

"Jess okay, Beth? That was a nasty cut."

"She was walking all right on the prom, just limping a bit."

"Oh, by the way," said Jamie, "can you tell your friend with the dog that dogs aren't allowed on this beach in the summer? Not between May and September, actually. She'll have to go farther down towards Hove. Gramps asked me to tell you."

"Oh, Rollo's all right," said Beth. "He never goes on the beach. He belongs to Maureen, the lady next door to us. He just guards her beach hut all day. He's really old."

"That's funny. Gramps said he saw a girl with a dog come up off the beach last evening and go into your beach hut. Maybe he made a mistake. He doesn't usually, but he's getting a bit old, too. Can you tell her anyway?"

"Okay. See you, Jamie!" But by the time Beth reached the beach hut, she was so hungry that she'd forgotten Jamie's message. "Quick, give me a sandwich!" she called out to Holly, "I'll faint in a minute."

Holly had already put out the deck chairs and had started eating. She passed a sandwich to Beth, who flopped down beside her.

After she'd finished a whole round of egg and cress sandwiches, Beth said, "Phew! That's better. I can think again now. Oh, I've just remembered. I've got to give Maureen a message. Jamie said to tell her that she mustn't take Rollo on the beach."

"Rollo never goes on the beach; he couldn't have said that. What did he actually say?"

"I don't remember exactly. Not absolutely word for word. It doesn't matter anyway. He just said could we tell our friend that dogs aren't allowed on the beach at the moment."

"But why did he say 'our friend'? I'm sure he knows Maureen. What else did he say?"

"I told you. You go and ask him if you don't believe me. Is there anything else to eat?" Beth opened a bottle of lemonade she found in the picnic basket.

"All right, I will then," said Holly, getting up from her deck chair.

"No, wait a sec. He did say something else, I've just remembered. He said his grandpa had asked him to give us the message because he'd seen a girl with a dog coming off the beach and going into our beach hut yesterday."

"He said WHAT? *A girl with a dog?* Don't you realise what this means? It was Marjorie! Marjorie and Peter. It just had to be. What are we doing wasting time eating?" Holly grabbed the basket and put it inside the beach hut. "Come in quickly and close the doors. Jenny could be back any minute!"

"This is stupid. It's hot and sunny; we can't close the doors." Beth stayed sitting in her deck chair, drinking lemonade.

"Come *on!*" Holly grabbed Beth's hand, pulled her into the beach hut, and shut the doors.

They sat down opposite each other on the yellow box benches.

Beth swung her feet impatiently and began to drum her fingers on the little table in an exaggerated movement. "So how long do we sit here then?" she asked. "I'm still hungry. Let's have the bananas."

"Oh no, Rollo's sniffing around outside; I can hear him. I hope he doesn't get the door open." Holly got up and knocked on the door. "Go away, Rollo, there's a good dog!"

The sniffing stopped, but only for a moment. The dog was apparently nudging its head against the doors, which moved slightly, and then the sniffing began again.

"This is hopeless," said Holly. "He'll have the doors open in a minute. Rollo, *please* be a good dog and go away." She sat down again with an exasperated sigh.

Beth said, "It's gone very quiet." It did seem quieter, but someone must have had a radio playing somewhere nearby because they could hear faint strains of music. It sounded like a brass band. Beth went over to the doors and listened. "I thought you weren't allowed radios on the prom. Anyway, I think Rollo's gone. Now can I have a banana?"

Holly sighed again and handed her one from the picnic basket. "You know what's going to happen?" she whispered. Why was she whispering, she wondered? There was no one to hear them. "Jenny's going to come back and open the doors, and we'll never get to see Marjorie again. We can't make it happen, you know. Perhaps it never will again and then we'll never know who Marjorie is. If only Mrs. Hawkes-Lewis hadn't died!"

"Why are you whispering?" said Beth, also in a whisper. "We're not in church or the library or anything."

Holly didn't answer, she wasn't sure herself. Minutes ticked by; the beach hut was becoming very hot. They sat there without speaking, but whoever had the radio must be carrying it towards them since the music was growing louder.

Then, "Who's Rollo?" said a small voice outside. "Good boy, Peter. I told you they'd come back, didn't I? I told you they wouldn't go away for ever and ever and not even say goodbye, didn't I, Peter? Shall we knock? Yes?"

It was Marjorie.

12

She was standing there in the glistening brightness, her white woollen knitted coat buttoned up against the breeze and a crocheted hat pulled down tightly over her hair. The sound of the Salvation Army band was growing gradually nearer. They had heard it, thought Holly; they'd heard the music. How extraordinary they had thought it was a radio! It was nothing like a radio.

In the vast blueness of the sky, a single gull wheeled and swooped, its almost human cry mingling with the sound of the singers on the prom.

"You've come back—I told them you would!" Marjorie looked ecstatically happy. "Dulcie said when you didn't come back last year, we'd never see you again." *Last year?* Holly and Beth looked at each other. What was she talking about? "But you're my friends and you said you'd come back. No, Peter, naughty dog."

The little fox terrier had run into the beach hut, rummaged around under the table and found a discarded biscuit.

"Peter, you weren't invited in; that's very naughty." Marjorie tried to sound cross, but when Peter sat down in front of them wagging his tail, they all laughed. "It's Josh's fault," said Marjorie. "He was here yesterday, and he gave Peter a Petit Beurre biscuit. He likes those. Gosh, have you been *bathing?*" She suddenly noticed that Holly and

Beth were both wearing swimsuits. Although she'd become used to the strangeness of these, quite unlike anything seen in her time, she looked amazed. "You're *so* lucky. Mother won't let me bathe yet. She says 'cast not a clout till May be out' and we're only halfway through May. Does your mother know? Doesn't she mind?"

"But it's Aug—" Beth began, when Holly quickly interrupted.

"She says it's okay if we don't stay in too long. It's because we live here, you see. Some people actually swim in the winter when it's freezing cold. Mostly old ladies. They've got a sort of club."

Marjorie burst out laughing. "Old ladies bathing in the winter? That's so funny! Perhaps they have little stoves in their bathing machines to get warm by when they come out. But I don't expect they have bathing machines on the beach in winter."

"Oh, I think they just go in off the beach," Holly said. "They're used to it. Are your friends on the beach now?"

"Yes, some of them. Come on, let's go and find them. Dulcie will be *so* surprised when she sees you."

"Okay. Just a sec." Holly grabbed Beth's arm and, while Marjorie was playing with Peter outside, whispered, "Bring your fleece—oh, and your sarong. We may need them." Then she carefully closed the beach hut doors behind them.

"Dulcie came down in the train this morning with Mother and me," Marjorie told them as they started off towards the West Pier. "Josh and Amelia are here, and two of Amelia's brothers, Tom and Bertie. They're twins. Oh, and Mia's friend, Tallulah, and her little sisters. Tallulah's such a funny name. Do you know anyone called Tallulah?"

"There's a Tabitha in my class at school," said Beth. They were half walking, half running along the prom with Peter bouncing ahead of them.

"Tabitha's a cat's name!" Marjorie laughed. "Oh, can you bring your cat costume next time you come? Holly said you've got one. I'd love to see it."

Beth gave Holly one of her looks. "I'll see if I can find it," she said.

By now they were within a few yards of the Salvation Army band. The sunlight was reflected in the shining brass of the band's instruments and the singing of the large crowd that had gathered rose joyfully into the clear air. The sound shimmered; it hung momentarily above their heads and then disappeared up into the blue sky. *How strange,* Holly thought. She'd never *seen* sound before; she wondered if Beth and Marjorie had seen it, too.

She could easily make out the words of the hymn the people were singing and the music was tremendous:

"Come, let us sing of a wonderful love,

Tender and true,

Out of the heart of the Father above,

Streaming to me and to you."

"Come on, let's join in," said Marjorie. "I know this one, do you? It's quite jolly and everyone's so gloomy in London because of the war, especially after last week when..."

Her words were lost in the crescendo of sound from the French horns.

So they stood there, Peter sitting dutifully at Marjorie's feet, as they sang from hymn sheets that had been hastily passed to them with smiles of welcome.

What a strange moment it was. It seemed almost outside time; not 1915—the year it now so obviously must be—and certainly not 2001, but somehow for all time. It was as if they had become part of a painting in a picture gallery, a moment caught forever on canvas. People would come and look at the picture and say, "Oh, how nice. I remember when it was like that. Look how happy the people are! You can almost hear the music." And they would smile at each other and sigh, saying, "Do you remember when...?" or "Weren't you wearing that blue dress?" and lots of little, happy things would be recalled.

But the singing now was very real and very heartfelt. Whatever tragedy had happened the week before, and in spite of the fear and sadness of the war, there still had to be joy and music and praise. It was something everyone needed, deep down, without even having to think about it. The scruffy, barefoot children, some clutching their mothers' hands; the smart ladies and gentlemen in neat hats and gloves; old people with lined and care-worn faces, but still with joy and hope in their eyes. Perhaps it was the music. Perhaps it was simply the comfort the words were giving them.

A large woman in a faded green serge dress, partly covered by a dirty, striped apron, turned to smile at the children as they started to sing. Her brown felt hat sported a grubby, orange flower which drooped slightly over the brim. The veins stood out on her big hands as she held the hymn sheet and there was dirt under her nails, but her eyes were deep blue and her wrinkled old face lit up when she saw the children. *How beautiful she is,* thought Holly; and then, how absurd, for how could she be?

An elderly gentleman in a cream blazer stooped to pat Peter. He had on a boater with a wide ribbon round it, and he carried a walking stick of twisted, shiny wood. "Good little fellow, good boy," he murmured, and Peter responded with an affectionate lick.

As they reached the last verse, the band and the congregation were on the move again. A few people left, but more joined in as they began to march towards Hove.

"We'd better go," said Marjorie, grabbing Beth's hand. "The others'll be wondering where I am. But that was fun, wasn't it? Look at Peter's tail wagging—he loves music. He likes to dance, too, like me. Go on, Peter, show my friends!"

Marjorie held up her hands and clapped, and Peter was up on his hind legs doing a little dance, looking for all the world like a circus dog.

They skipped along the prom with Peter running behind them. And then suddenly, just in a moment, a fleeting second really, Holly felt—no, she knew, though she didn't know why—that this would be the last time they would be able to go back to Marjorie's time. How would it end? Would they just walk away from it, with no one ever believing them that it had happened at all? Mr. Edwards did. No one had ever believed him. How she wished she'd heard the end of his story! How did he get back to his own time, and why could he never return to 1876? But there was still so much to discover here, now; they must make the most of every minute.

"They're over on the other side of the pier," called out Marjorie. "Near the wall. Because the tide's high. I expect Dulcie'll come to meet us. Oh look, there she is!"

Dulcie was running towards them, her short, fair, curly hair bouncing in the breeze. She was wearing a mauve knitted coat similar in style to Marjorie's but without a hat.

"Where've you *been?*" she called out. "I've been waiting for ages and...oh, *waterspouts!* You've got Holly and Beth with you!" Dulcie's colourful expressions were a source of great amusement to her friends.

When the children reached the little group on the beach, they were all sitting on the pebbles staring out to sea, with the exception of the two little girls, Tallulah's sisters, who were being helped by their nursemaid to build a castle out of the flatter stones. Josh was shielding his eyes and talking animatedly. He stood up when he saw them coming.

"I say! Marjorie was right—you have come back! We're going to have lunch in a minute. Care to join us?"

"What are you looking at, Josh?" asked Marjorie. She shielded her eyes too against the glare. "I can't see anything. Oh yes, we'd love to. I mean Holly and Beth will, won't you? But Josh, I still can't see anything."

"It's almost out of sight now. But there was a ship on the horizon. Black smoke was pouring from its funnels. At least we're not sure if it was from its funnels; maybe it was the ship itself. It looked bad."

Josh had grown up. His voice had broken and he was inches taller. It quite alarmed Holly; she had seen him only a few days ago, in her time, and he'd changed so much.

"We were thinking of the poor old Lusitania last week," he said. "All those people drowned! Torpedoed so near the end of her journey. She had just eight miles to go. The Bosch are murderers. Murderers of innocent women and children."

"Yes, and it sank in just twenty-one minutes. It said so in the newspaper," put in Tom. "It said: 'Fourteen hundred people feared drowned.' I wish I could join up. I'd like to show 'em!"

"If this war lasts," said Josh, "I'm going to join Algie at the front; they're sure to have him after he's eighteen next month. I want to *do* something. But right now,"—he had a knack of suddenly changing from the serious to the lighthearted—"I don't know about you, but I'm hungry." The familiar broad smile spread across his face. "What say we start on the picnic? The mothers will be ages visiting Great Aunt Harriet, and I'm sure they won't mind. Can we eat, Nursie?"

He addressed the little girls' nursemaid, already tiring from her castle building.

"I think, Master Josh, that it is a very good idea. But don't you call me 'Nursie'! My name's Nurse May. Please remember that."

"Right ho, Nursie. Come on, boys, let's get the picnic baskets. I say, just a sec, though; did you hear the rhyme about Charlie Chaplin? It goes like this:

'Oh, the moon shines bright on Charlie Chaplin,

His boots are crackling for want of blackening

And his little baggy trousers they want mending

Before they send him to the Dardanelles.'"

Bertie started to giggle. He stood up, grabbed Nurse May's hat, put his hands in his trouser pockets, and set off towards the sea, feet pointed outwards in the manner of Charlie Chaplin. Amelia was shaking with laughter.

"Bertie, don't be an idiot!" said Amelia. "Mother'll kill you if you get your clothes all wet."

"Who's Charlie Chaplin?" whispered Beth, leaning close to Holly.

Holly put her finger to her lips, and then, in a moment of distraction when Tom, determined that his brother shouldn't be the only one to get his boots wet, had scrambled down the stony beach after Bertie, she whispered back, "He was a comic actor, a long time ago. He was very famous."

To her horror, she saw Amelia giving her a puzzled look. Had she heard? But then her brothers were back, both with wet boots and in fits of laughter, chased up the beach by Tallulah, and the moment passed.

Soon, two big picnic baskets that had been carried down from a small tent, skillfully pitched with tent poles pushed between the stones, were set down in front of them.

"Who's going to serve us, then?" said Amelia, as she opened the lid of the first basket. "I desire to be waited on. It *is* my birthday, you know!"

"We had not forgotten, my lady," said Josh with a bow. "We'll call the maid. I know! Let's agitate the communicator!" There were shrieks of laughter from Amelia as Josh pulled an imaginary bell-pull.

"Don't make fun of my daddy." Marjorie looked cross, put her arms round Peter, and buried her head in his fur.

Whatever was she talking about?

"I'm not," said Amelia. "Your daddy's lovely. He's cuddly. My father's stiff and proud like a soldier."

"That's because he is a soldier." Josh turned to Holly and Beth. "Mia's father fought in South Africa. He was at the siege of Mafeking. He won lots of medals."

"Yes, but he's too old to fight now," said Amelia. "Mother says she's pleased. She says it's bad enough having three sons at the Front."

The sandwiches were being passed round now; there were ham and tomato, egg and cucumber, and a biscuit tin filled with banana and jam sandwiches for afterwards.

"What did Josh mean when he said 'agitate the communicator'?" Beth asked Marjorie. "And why is it making fun of your dad? We don't understand."

"It was funny really," said Marjorie. "I just don't like people making fun of Daddy." She took a ham and tomato sandwich and laid it carefully in her lap. "You see, we were all at Auntie Hettie's and Uncle Percy's—that's Mr. and Mrs. Hawkes-Lewis, Josh's parents— in St. Aubyn's," a shiver of excitement ran down Holly's spine, "for Sunday lunch just after Easter. Daddy said—just for fun, because he always says it at our house—'Shall I agitate the communicator?' Ring the bell for the maid, you see. So he did, and…"

"Sarah came in with the tomato soup," put in Josh. "She's our new maid, and she was feeling a bit nervous. The bell wouldn't stop ringing; it was stuck or something. I don't know what she thought, but she suddenly dropped the whole tureen of soup and ran. The soup went everywhere! Mother ran after her and found her sobbing in the passage, and still the bell wouldn't stop."

"I know it was wicked of me," said Amelia, "but I was laughing so much the tears were streaming down my cheeks and Mrs. Hawkes-Lewis said, very sternly, 'I think we had better retire to the drawing room while I speak to Mrs. Hewitt'—she's their housekeeper— 'about this. Control yourself, my gal. This is most unladylike behaviour.' And then…"

"The bell went on ringing for ages," added Josh, "and the more it rang and the more serious our mothers got, the more we laughed!"

"Daddy thought it was funny, too," said Marjorie, "but I think he felt sorry for Sarah. He kept saying sorry to Uncle Percy who looked very stern and serious and muttered 'quite all right, my dear fellow, quite all right. Not your fault at all.'"

"It was a spiffing day," put in Bertie. "All that tomato soup looked like blood on the carpet. We'd never had a better Sunday lunch."

"Yes, I'm sure I'll never forget it as long as I live. It was *so* funny!" said Amelia.

Holly caught Beth's eye. Was she, too, remembering Roland Hawkes-Lewis's words? They came to her so clearly now that he might have been standing there and speaking them himself. 'No, I'm afraid she never told us the story about the bells. Sadly, it has died with her.' Then Holly looked at the young, vibrant, red-haired girl, laughing even now as she told the story her grandson would never hear, and she thought of the quiet bungalow with the open book by the sofa bed and the half-drunk glass of water. No, it can't have happened; how could Amelia have died only last Sunday, an old lady of one hundred and one?

Holly saw that there were tears in Beth's eyes. Marjorie had noticed and a look of grave concern spread over her face. She put a hand on Beth's arm.

"Beth, why are you crying? What's the matter? Are you all right?"

"Oh, it's nothing." Beth wiped away the tears with her sleeve. "I was just thinking of...of..." she was searching her brain for an excuse, "all those people on the Lucy...um...the Lucythingy and of all those people who'd drowned and..."

"Golly, did you know someone on the Lusitania?" put in Josh. "That's awful. And here we are having fun and laughing. I say, that's too bad of us."

"Oh no, it's okay," Holly quickly took control. "We didn't actually know anybody. It's just Beth. She gets emotional. She likes being emotional. You're fine now, aren't you, Beth? She's worse when she's hungry. Look, have another sandwich." She thrust an egg sandwich at Beth who gave Holly another of her 'looks.' But her tears had stopped, and she was smiling. The happy mood of the party was restored.

The sandwiches were delicious, on crusty brown bread.

"Mother had them made in the hotel kitchen," said Josh. "She's very fussy about fillings. Actually, she's awfully bossy when she goes to the kitchen; the cooks and everbody are quite frightened of her. I try to keep out of the way."

He took two stone bottles of ginger beer out of the picnic basket and passed them to Bertie and Tom. "Here, you can unscrew the tops of these. The girls need cups; we can just drink from the bottles."

Enamel mugs filled to the brim with ginger beer were passed to Holly and Beth first, as guests to the picnic, and then to Amelia, Tallulah, Marjorie and Dulcie. Tallulah's little sisters had to be content with milk.

They ate in silence for a few minutes enjoying the picnic, pushing their mugs down into the pebbles to steady them while they ate. Only Ducie's managed to tip sideways and spill.

"Oh, waterspouts!" she said again.

When half the sandwiches had been eaten and the mothers had still not returned, Josh stood up.

"I have an announcement to make. As man of the house, so to speak, it has fallen to me to do the honours. Let's all raise our glasses—or bottles, or cups—to Amelia. Happy Birthday, Mia!"

He walked a few steps down towards the sea, held up his arms and shouted, so that everyone anywhere near them would hear, "Happy... Birthday... Mia! Fifteen today!"

The few families seated near them on the beach joined in the toast, calling out, "Happy Birthday, Mia!" Several small children came running over. One little lad of about five years old held out a yellow balloon to her.

"'Ere y'are, miss. It's my birthday, too, but you can 'ave it!" He ran quickly back to his mother before Amelia could stop him.

Marjorie walked over to the little beach tent and came back holding a box wrapped in white paper. She gave it to Amelia, who was holding the string of the balloon tightly as the breeze tugged at it.

"This is from me and Dulcie. We bought it together. We hope you like it. Daddy said you would; he said he'd like it."

Amelia took the box with a big smile and, to the delight of Tallulah's little sisters, handed the balloon to their nursemaid for them to play with. She tore off the paper quickly.

"Oh, I love it! It's crystallised ginger. Thank you, thank you very much." She gave Marjorie, and then Dulcie, a hug. "But you must share it with me, then it's special." She opened the box, and they each took a piece.

Josh sat close to Amelia while the presents were brought to her. Tom gave her a little red wooden musical box with a flower painted on the lid; Bertie, pleading poverty, presented her with the latest copy of The Rainbow comic with a picture of Tiger Tim on the front cover and a little paper bag of jelly babies. Amelia, laughing, gave each of them a kiss, assuring them the presents were lovely and just what she wanted.

Tallulah sat on the other side of Amelia, the skirt of her brown serge dress pulled up to her knees, showing shiny brown button boots, now scuffed by the stones. She wore a wide cream leather belt with a little purse attached to it.

"I've got a present for you, too," she said, as she opened the belt pocket. She handed her friend a tiny package, wrapped in tissue paper and tied with a silver ribbon. Amelia carefully untied the ribbon and opened the paper.

"Oh, it's so pretty!" she said. "I shall wear it straight away."

A little star-shaped hair clip, made of some kind of shiny metal, lay in the tissue paper. She pushed back a crinkly strand of her long red hair and fastened it with the little clip. It caught the sun and sparkled, as her eyes sparkled. She was enjoying her birthday.

Josh was holding something behind his back. Now he brought it out and, blushing slightly, handed her his gift. It looked like a book. It was wrapped in brown paper and tied in pink string, fastened with a bow. She smiled at Josh, a happy, excited smile, as she carefully untied the string, then rolled it up into a little ball and put it in her pocket. She unwrapped the paper slowly, as if she wanted the moment of expectation to last a little longer.

It was a book. The buff coloured cover had strange patterns around the edge and an Eastern design on the front. The writing on the book looked as if it was in an Arabic script, but the words inside were in English.

"Oh, it's beautiful!" she said, as she opened the pages of the book. "What lovely pictures. Oh, and the verses are so beautiful."

It was a book of Eastern poetry, and the illustrations were in wonderful soft colours, but it had the strangest title. The cover read: The Rubaiyat of Omar Khyam.

"You pronounce it 'Roo—by—at,'" said Josh, "of 'Oh -ma—ky—am.' It's Persian."

"Oh, Josh, it's so lovely. Where did you get it? I shall treasure it always."

Josh beamed. He pushed his floppy black hair away from his eyes self-consciously and blushed even more deeply.

"I bought it yesterday at Friends' Bookshop in Western Road. It was the only copy they had. I'm so pleased you like it. I wasn't sure. I thought, well—I just wasn't sure. Read us something from it."

"All right." She cleared her throat. "I'll start at the beginning. 'Awake! For morning in the Bowl of Night, has flung the stone that puts the Stars to Flight. And lo! The Hunter of the East has caught the Sultan's turret in a Noose of Light.'" Blushing herself now, she leaned over and gave Josh a kiss. Bertie and Tom nudged one another and exchanged knowing looks.

Marjorie said, "Please, can I have a look at it? I promise I'll be very, very careful." Amelia passed it to her. Every page had a decorated border, and there were many coloured pictures like watercolours painted in an Eastern style.

"Oh, I'd just love to have this book," sighed Marjorie as she took it carefully in both hands. "Can I read another bit from it?" She was turning several pages now. "I love this picture of the courtyard and the fountain and the old buildings. It's so... so *old* looking. It looks like a picture in a fairy story, as if something magic's going to happen. Listen: 'Think, in this battered cara...' what's this word? Oh yes, 'caravan—ser–ai...,'" she pronounced it carefully, syllable by syllable, "'whose doorways are alternate Night and Day, How Sultan after Sultan with his pomp, Abode his hour or two, and went his way.' Aren't those lovely words? I'm going to ask Mother and Daddy for this book for my next birthday."

Holly and Beth looked at each other, feeling uncomfortable they had no present for Amelia. But there was nothing they could do. Or was there?

13

To Holly's amazement, Beth suddenly jumped up and clapped her hands.

"Listen," she said, "I want to say something." Then, turning to Amelia she began, "We're really sorry we haven't got a present for you. We didn't know it was your birthday. But I'm going to be like the Good Fairy at Sleeping Beauty's Christening and grant you a very special wish. The wish is that—"

Everyone was looking at Beth. Holly's heart was pounding. Whatever was Beth going to say? She mustn't, she really mustn't try to change history. Holly kept thinking of Mr. Edwards's words, "You're there by grace." She thought that at last she was beginning to understand what he meant.

"You will live right into the next century," announced Beth. "You will live to be one hundred and one years old."

Everyone laughed and clapped.

Amelia said, "Thank you for that special birthday wish. I don't think it will happen, but wouldn't it be fun if it did? I wonder what it will be like in 2001? Perhaps we'll all live in glass houses, and people will be flying to the moon. Maybe it will be just like catching a train to London now. I know, perhaps someone will have invented a machine to do all my sums for me then I won't have to do all that horrible long division any more."

Holly held her breath. What would Beth say?

She never had the chance. At that moment, the yellow balloon, which Tallulah's sisters had been playing with, took off in a gust of wind towards the pier. The little girls screamed in dismay. The balloon floated over the railings and was on its way to the roof of the bandstand when its string became entangled in the metal balustrade, holding it fast.

"We'll get it back, don't you worry," said Josh, leaping to his feet. "Who's coming with me? Mia, are you coming?"

"No, I think I'll stay here and read my book; I'll leave the heroics to you. Besides, Mother will be back soon. She might be cross if I wasn't here, and anyway, I'm sure the balloon will have flown away by the time you get there."

Bertie and Tom were deep in Amelia's copy of The Rainbow, and Tallulah thought she should stay with her little sisters.

"I'll come!" said Marjorie. "Holly and Beth'll come too, won't you? Are you coming, Dulcie?"

Nurse May looked anxious. "I'm not sure about this, Master Josh. Piers can be dangerous places. I don't know what Miss Marjorie's mother will say, but I think Miss Dulcie should wait here for her mother. She's very particular."

"Nursie," said Josh, "I give you my solemn promise that I will bring all the girls safely back. Holly and Beth can't ask their mother because she's not here, but I shall guard them and Marjorie with my life. Peter can come too as our protector. Operation Balloon will now commence."

And so, much against Nurse May's better judgment and to the anguish of the deserted Dulcie, the four of them and Peter set off for the West Pier. Holly and Beth wrapped their sarongs around their waists as they hurried along. Their twenty-first century swimsuits, which were somehow acceptable on the beach, might appear a little indecent to the ladies and gentlemen promenading on the pier.

They ran through the open gates, past the stalls selling jellied eels and mugs of tea, and were running along the deck, anxious to get to the balloon before the wind whisked it away, when Marjorie suddenly stopped.

"Don't you love that feeling of excitement when you first step on the deck—like this—and you can see the sea churning away so far down below that it makes you feel dizzy?" Marjorie was standing with her feet tightly together and staring through the small gaps in the decking where the sea did indeed churn and swirl in the wind and the currents created by the supporting structures under the pier.

"Mother hates it," she was saying as Josh took her hand and hurried her towards the bandstand and the balustrade to which, thankfully, the balloon was still attached. "She doesn't like coming on the pier at all. It's so lovely to come with you and Peter."

"Right," Josh said as they all arrived at the bandstand, "now all we have to do is carefully disentangle the string, like so…"

Josh was holding the string just below the balloon with one hand and tugging at the entrapped end when Peter suddenly, and for no apparent reason, set up a loud barking. The string, released at last, slipped through Josh's fingers. The balloon shot away from him in a sudden downwards gust that blew it out onto the surface of the sea where a wave caught it and hurled it towards the shore.

They all rushed to the railings.

"I don't believe it!" cried Josh. "The wind's changed directions. Look, the balloon's floating towards the beach. Tom! Bertie!" he yelled, cupping his hands, while the girls jumped up and down and waved frantically. "Get it, quick—it's coming in!"

The two little girls, who had been watching the rescue of their treasured balloon, ran to Tom and Bertie and, pulling the boys' sleeves and with much protestation from Nurse May, dragged them towards the sea. Tom flung off his boots and waded in, revelling in the chance to get really wet, and just as another wave was about to snatch the balloon from his reach, he caught the string.

Josh and the girls clapped and cheered from the pier, but Peter was still barking.

"Peter, what's the matter?" Marjorie leaned down and took his collar. "You must stop barking; people won't like it. What *is* the matter?"

To Marjorie's dismay, Peter pulled himself away from her and ran to a small white-painted hut next to the bandstand. He put his paws up on the door, whining and barking.

"Peter, come away! What are you doing?" Marjorie was trying to take his collar again when the door opened a crack and a man's head appeared. He had greasy black hair and an untidy beard. He looked very angry.

"Call off your dog!" he shouted, and then muttered something in a foreign language. "Or I vill call ze… ze… poleece. He is… a bad dog… I say he is…"

Marjorie was on the verge of tears and trying desperately to control her beloved Peter, helped by Holly and Beth.

"Look here," said Josh, "don't you call our dog bad. What are you doing in there anyway? That's the attendant's hut, and you're not the attendant. I know him."

The man flung open the door, gave them a brief fearful stare, rushed off down the pier past the bandstand and jumped over a padlocked gate, which shut off the end section where construction work on a new concert hall had been started.

This time Marjorie held tight to Peter, who was ready to follow. She dried her tears and hugged him. "You're a good dog, and he's a bad man," she said. "Good boy, Peter."

Beth was staring towards the end of the pier. "Look!" she said, "Look at that! They're still building this part. Look at all those arches. There must be... one, two, three... eight. Yes, eight arches. Mum'll love to hear about this."

Holly grabbed her arm, saying loudly, "But Mum knows about it, *doesn't she? She's seen it before, hasn't she?*" Beth glared at her.

Josh, for once, was saying nothing, but looked very thoughtful. Then he said, "I know that man. I've seen his picture in the newspaper. He's a German spy. At least, that's what the police think. And didn't you hear his accent? He was talking in a foreign language to himself, too. It's him, I'm sure it is."

"What do you mean, he's a spy?" asked Holly. "What did it say in the papers?"

"He was caught taking photos along the seafront and by the Palace Pier," said Josh. "He was acting suspiciously and some people reported it to the police. They caught him, but he wouldn't say anything and somehow he managed to get away from them and escaped. But they had his camera, and he dropped a piece of card with all sorts of figures on it and diagrams. The police think he was taking photos of possible landing places for an enemy invasion."

"Then we've got to let the police know he's here," said Marjorie. "Now look how clever Peter is; he caught a German spy."

"No, wait," said Josh. "We've got to think out a plan of action. If we go now to tell the police..."

"Or the army," said Beth.

"Or the navy," said Holly.

"Yes, all right, or the army or the navy, we'll lose him. We'll have to track him, and then lure him into somewhere—like the attendant's hut—where we can lock him in. There was a padlock hanging off that door. If we could just get Peter to..."

"No!" said Marjorie. "The man might hurt him. We can't use Peter."

"All right, so we need to get some grown-ups to help. But first, let's see if we can find out where he's got to because he can't get off the pier from that end, not without a boat, and it's awfully dangerous, too, because of the construction work for the concert hall."

There were very few people on the pier that day; the gusty wind was not conducive to sitting in a deck chair and the bandstand was not in use. There was no one working on the new building because it was a Sunday, but just past the bandstand was a small kiosk with elegant white wooden fretwork around its windows and door. Over the door a sign read "Gypsy Marigold Merry. Fortune Teller."

"We could try her," Josh suggested. "She might even tell us what he's up to. But let's have a look over the gate first. We've not seen him come back, and I've been watching all the time. He's got to be still over there."

"I'm scared," said Beth. "Suppose he's got a gun or something? You told Nurse May you'd guard us with your life."

"And so I shall." Josh put his arm round Beth's shoulders. "Don't worry, we won't do anything dangerous."

They all leaned over the metal gate, watching for movement of any kind. The new building was eight-sided, as Beth had spotted, and with all those arches there were plenty of places to hide. But eventually, the man would have to come out and climb back over the gate in order to get off the pier.

"I know," said Josh. "Beth and I'll go in to Gypsy Marigold to ask for her help, and Marjorie, you and Holly wait outside to keep watch. Knock on the door immediately if you see anything."

"I want to stay outside with Marjorie," said Beth. "You and Holly go in. It looks spooky."

"Right ho. I just thought that as Holly's a bit older, she could be in charge of spy-watch duty."

"But Beth and I have Peter," said Marjorie. "He'll look after us and bark if the man comes back. We'll be very good spy-watchers, won't we, Beth?"

"All right," agreed Josh, his hand on the doorknob, "but make sure you knock just as soon as you see or hear anything at all suspicious."

The door opened on to a room that was in almost total darkness. The only sources of light were a big crystal ball that glowed whitely, illuminating the strange face of Gypsy Marigold, and a small oil lamp with a red glass shade. On a perch high up near the roof was a black bird, about the size of a small raven, swinging on its perch. Its bright eyes caught the light from the oil lamp.

"Fortune," it croaked. "Tell your fortune. Only sixpence. Shut the door."

The face behind the crystal ball broke into a toothless smile. The crimson scarf tied around the gypsy's forehead was edged with yellow gold coins and a mass of coloured beads hung around her rather scraggy neck.

"Well, come in, my dears. And have you got a silver sixpence for an old gypsy woman who'll tell you all you want to know?"

A little tinkly bell sounded as the door shut behind them. A feeling of panic was seizing Holly; she grabbed Josh's arm and held on tightly to him.

"We haven't got any money," said Josh. "We just need your help. There's a man on the end of the pier and we think he's a German spy."

Gypsy Marigold flung her head back and cackled with laughter. "German spy? Out there? We think the young gen'leman's imagining things, don't we, Methuselah?" She was addressing the mynah bird on the swinging perch. "What shall we do, my lovely? Shall we help the young master and miss? But he don't have a sixpence, do 'e?"

Josh was beginning to feel a little unnerved by now and was on the point of leaving when the mynah bird shrieked, "No sixpence. Tell him! Tell him! Shut the door."

"All right, my lovely." The old woman stood up and stroked the bird's head. The light from the crystal ball shone on her shabby full skirt. Now Holly could see it was dark green with a pattern in faded gold of moons and stars. Her frilly white blouse under the weight of the beads was dirty and crumpled.

"Let's go," whispered Holly, tugging at Josh's arm. "I don't like it here. Let's go."

"Go?" The gypsy had heard. "Go, before you hear your fortune? You want my help. I have to know what the future holds for you. Sit down here, young man. You will be first. You're safe here with Gypsy Marigold." She placed her hands on the glowing crystal ball and muttered some incantations under her breath. "Ah yes," she said, as she stared at the ball, "I see a journey. A journey across the sea."

"They always say that," whispered Josh to Holly. "All gypsies say it."

"A journey with many people. I see smoke, smoke and fire…"

"That's it!" said Josh, "I'm going to join up. When, though? Will it be soon? I'm not quite sixteen—"

"Ah, so young, so young. But there will be a journey." The gypsy closed her eyes for a moment, and the light from the ball dimmed.

"But what about the German spy? Where is he? Will we catch him?" Josh was leaning forward, trying to see the image in the crystal ball.

"Wait, wait!" She moved her hands around the ball, which began to glow more brightly again. The mynah bird's perch creaked eerily in the near darkness, and the flame of the oil lamp hissed.

"I see a boat. And a man, a man with a beard... it is very hazy now. The man is on the very end of...of...it is this pier. He is there on the end. But no, perhaps... ah, let me have the young miss to sit down. My crystal ball will reveal his secret hiding place through her."

Josh got up, and tentatively Holly took his place. The wooden chair was warm where Josh had been sitting, but the room felt cold. The old woman placed her hands on the ball once more and her crooked fingers caressed the now brightly glowing crystal, casting moving shadows on the pitched wooden roof. As Holly's eyes grew accustomed to the darkness, she began to notice other things she'd not seen before. A pack of cards lay on the chenille tablecloth, cards with strange and frightening pictures on them. The pack was cut and some lay face downwards, but Holly recognised them as Tarot cards. She'd seen them in an old shop off the Lanes where she and her mother had been shopping. Katy had warned her never to play with cards like that, that they were evil and could affect your mind. Holly tried not to look at them and concentrated on the crystal ball, but a growing fear was mounting in her. Somewhere in the darkness behind the gypsy's chair, something moved. Holly was sure she caught the glint of a pair of eyes staring at her.

"What is your name, miss? Holly? Well, Holly, Christmas Holly, you will go on a journey..." she began. Josh winked at Holly. But then the gypsy stopped. She stared at Holly and then at the ball.

"I do not understand what the crystal ball reveals to me. It does not lie!" She looked agitated. The mynah bird swung faster on its perch, squawking quietly as the gypsy bent closer to the ball, her face almost touching it. "The future time and now, it is all—" She lifted her head and stared at Holly. "It is all confused."

She breathed on the ball and rubbed it with her grubby sleeve. "I do not understand," she repeated. "Your future, it is now. The ball tells me so. It shows me strange things I do not know. It shows me—"

Holly stood up and grabbed Josh's hand. "Quick, let's go. That's a knock on the door, I'm sure it is."

Josh turned to open the door. It would not move. The gypsy seemed to be in some kind of trance, and the room was growing darker as the light from the crystal ball faded.

"We've got to get out—now!" Holly was frantic. The room was beginning to spin and a sick feeling was rising in her stomach. "Come on, Josh, lean on the door. We'll push together. Okay—NOW!"

The mynah bird let out a piercing shriek as light flooded into the room. Neither Holly nor Josh turned to look, but they heard the beat of its wings and felt the current of air from its flight as it swooped towards them. They slammed the door shut behind them just in time.

Holly collapsed on the deck, overcome by dizziness. Marjorie had her arms round her and was talking to her, but although she could see her lips moving, Holly could not hear her. Beth was frantically trying to pull her up; she was saying something, asking questions, so many questions, and pleading with her to move, but she couldn't move. And where was Josh?

At last, she managed to pull herself into a sitting position and put her head between her knees. She knew that was the right thing to do if you felt faint, but here at the far end of the pier the gaps between the deck boards were wider and the sight of the swirling sea far below only increased her nausea. If she stared down at the waves, she was sure she would lose consciousness, and then what would happen? Where would she be? Here, in 1915, or back in 2001? And what would happen to Beth? No, she must fight this awful feeling, she must hold on. The salty taste in her mouth was horrid, a warning that at any minute she might be sick. She must get up, get to the side, lean over....

Holly held on to Marjorie and Beth who were near to tears and then suddenly there was Josh, red in the face from running, holding a mug of cold water out to her. She could see his lips moving, urging her to drink. She took the mug with trembling hands and sipped slowly, as Jamie had told Jessica to do when she had cut her foot.

Gradually, the world began to come back into focus, and now she could hear them talking to her, the concern in their voices and their pleading for her to sit still until she felt better. Peter was trying to lick her face and had his paw on her arm.

The cold water was beginning to work and the dizziness was easing.

"It's all right. I'm okay." Holly was relieved to find she could still speak. She was afraid that maybe she really was in a dream, the sort when you try to call out and no sound comes. "I'll be all right now. I'll try to stand up."

She slowly got to her feet, helped by all three children. The breeze blew through her hair, and the scent of sea spray was beginning to revive her.

"I'll go to the railings a minute," she said, "just in case. I still feel a bit sick. I think I'll be all right, but just in case."

Josh held one of her arms and Marjorie and Beth took the other as they helped Holly to the railings. She took a deep breath, let it go slowly, then another. Her head was clearing.

Looking out across the sea, she could see no boats, no one was in the water and the beach was a long way off, yet just for a second, she had the distinct feeling someone was watching her, looking straight at her from the sea. It was very odd. She turned around to look the other way, but there was no one near her, only an elderly couple about fifty yards away walking arm in arm towards the entrance. She must be imagining it, she told herself, but it was a very strong feeling.

And then suddenly Holly remembered why they were there and all other thoughts went out of her mind.

"Oh no!" she cried, "the German spy! He's probably got away by now. It's all my fault! I'm so sorry, I'm really sorry."

"He hasn't, I know he hasn't," said Marjorie. "Peter would have told us if he'd come back over the gate. He hates him. He'd have barked and barked. I know he would."

"Marjorie's right," said Josh. "We've got to assume he's still somewhere on the end of the pier. We've got to get help, and *not* from any gypsy fortuneteller, either. I say, but it was a bit rum in there, wasn't it? It's all made up, of course, but, well…"

"Look! Over there!" Mercifully, Beth interrupted Josh's thoughts. "There's someone there behind that pillar, the one with ladder against it. It's got to be him."

14

They all rushed to the gate. Peter started to growl in a most ferocious way for such a friendly dog. The man ran right across the half-built concert hall and disappeared behind some hoarding that had been constructed across one of the arches.

"We've lost him for now," said Josh. "He could stay in hiding there for as long as he likes—or until he gets hungry. We'll have to nab the first grown-up who comes along and ask them to get the police. I reckon we could risk—"

"No, look! Over there! We haven't lost him." It was Beth who once again had spotted movement. "He's climbing over the fence, and he's holding something. It looks like a piece of metal."

Peter set up a loud barking. The man had somehow managed to scale the high fence and jump to the ground, catching his coat on the way down so that a piece of torn black cloth hung on the top of the fence flapping in the breeze.

He saw the children and, to their horror, ran towards them waving an iron bar in the air and shouting, "Keep away, or I kill your dog. I vill kill him…" followed by a stream of angry German.

"That's done it," said Josh. "He's not going to get away with it this time, help or no help. Quick, through here!"

He pulled the girls through a gap in the windbreak running the length of the pier. They flattened themselves against the wooden wall, Marjorie coaxing Peter to be quiet. They heard the man run heavily past on the other side, footsteps echoing loudly on the wooden boards. About halfway along the windbreak, his steps began to slow; the weight of the iron bar must have dragged him down.

"Wait here," said Josh, "don't move, but if you see a grown-up, tell them what's happened. I can outrun old Kaiser Bill there any day."

And he was off, running lightly over the boards in his plimsolls, dodging between the gaps in the windbreak if he thought he'd been spotted.

Holly watched as he ran, shielding her eyes against the bright sun. Then suddenly, in the shimmering glare, she saw the pier was no longer new and freshly painted; it was just a shabby, rusty structure, ending abruptly in a narrow bridge that linked it to the shore.

She called out in terror, "Josh, look out! You're getting to the end. It's just a narrow walkway—look out!"

Marjorie seemed not to hear her as she held tight to Peter, but Beth looked frightened.

Then, just as Holly feared the worst, there was the pier back again in all its glory, continuing safely to the shore. She rubbed her eyes and blinked. What was happening? Was it the parallel lines coming together, the vanishing point in time Mrs. Howard had talked about? Would it happen again? Maybe they'd find themselves back in 2001 without returning to the beach hut at all, and Marjorie and her friends would just disappear. *That would be dreadful,* she thought; *it mustn't end like that!*

Her fearful thoughts were interrupted by a crash that vibrated through the deck, and a loud metallic clang as something hit the railings.

"What's happened?" cried Marjorie, "what's happened to Josh? What're we going to *do?*" She sounded very frightened but was the first to peep out from their hiding place.

Josh, with an expert rugby tackle, had felled the man and was now sitting on top of him. The iron bar had slipped from his hand and hit the railings as he landed heavily on the deck. The three girls, with Peter barking excitedly, ran towards Josh and his captive who were by now surrounded by a small crowd of people.

Holly caught hold of Beth and in an urgent whisper said, "Beth, we've got to get back to the beach hut. Really, now, as quickly as possible. We're losing it. I saw the old pier just now, just a bit of it, all shabby and rusty." She was nearly out of breath. "We're losing it— we've got to go!"

"I'm not going now!" Beth was horrified at Holly's demand. "This is brilliant fun, really exciting. We'll all get our names in the newspapers, and Josh is a hero. And anyway, I promised Marjorie I'd show her some of my dance steps. We can't possibly go yet. Come *on!*"

Marjorie had raced ahead with Peter, but Beth was determined to catch up. Holly kept running too now, afraid to stop and afraid to turn round in case of what she might see. Maybe, if she wanted it badly enough, they could stay in 1915 just a little longer. There was still so much to find out, so much they still didn't know. Why should it end now? But then she didn't know how it had started, or why.

So she kept running. The tide must have been going out, for even as she ran, she could hear the swish of the stones in the pull of the waves under the pier. Soon there would be a patch of sand below the pebbles.

In a moment, there she was beside Josh and the ever-growing crowd of spectators, all ready, no doubt, to restrain the prisoner should he try to escape. Coming towards them at a brisk walk was a tall lady in a herringbone tweed coat, fastened at the waist by a single button. With one hand, she held on to her wide-brimmed brown felt hat, which threatened to fly off in the breeze, and the other she had on the arm of a rather burly policeman.

"Crikey!" said Josh. "It's Mother, and she's brought a Bobby with her."

§ § § § §

Mrs. Hawkes-Lewis had arrived back at the beach along with Marjorie's mother just as four policemen were seen running along the prom in the direction of the pier. Nurse May, who had just heard the news from a passer-by, was beside herself: Master Josh, Miss Marjorie, and her friends were on the pier with a *dangerous criminal.* She couldn't leave the little girls, could she, ma'am? And there was Miss Amelia wanting to hurry off to the pier to find out what was happening, and Master Tom and Master Bertie would refuse to listen to reason and were at that very moment putting their boots back on ready to join her. Whatever was she to do?

Leaving Marjorie's mother to take charge of the distraught nurse and the other children, Mrs. Hawkes-Lewis had gathered up her skirts in a most unlikely manner and had almost run to the pier, reaching the entrance just as the police sergeant was instructing his officers to keep guard there while he went in pursuit of the suspect. She'd immediately confronted him and demanded that she accompany him in his duty, refusing to be deterred by his warnings of danger. Her son and his friends were involved, she'd told him, so danger was irrelevant.

And that was when Josh saw her, marching purposefully towards him and clutching her hat against the wind.

"Morris!" called out Josh's mother. "What ever is going on? Are the girls safe? What have you done?"

"That's torn it," said Josh, overheard by the whole crowd. "She only ever calls me Morris when she's cross." A ripple of laughter went through the crowd, and a moan from the prostrate German.

"Well, young fellow-me-lad, and what 'ave we got here?" The policeman, truncheon in hand, was standing over Josh. "Get up now, lad, and leave this to me. You've done a grand job. We've been after this one for a while."

Josh stood up, seizing the iron bar as he did so. He didn't want to leave anything to chance. The policeman hauled the dishevelled man to his feet.

"Heinrich Muntz," he said, as he clapped handcuffs on his prisoner—only he pronounced the name Henryk Moons—"I arrest you in the name of His Majesty, King George V, on suspicion of plotting against King and Country." Ignoring the formal warning that should be issued for an arrest, he continued, "And what have you got to say for yourself?"

Everyone waited expectantly in silence, but he hung his head and said nothing. Sergeant Watkins, for that was the policeman's name, blew his whistle loudly. Being unable to see over the heads of the crowd, the children could only hear the approaching footsteps as they echoed on the deck boards.

"Move along, please, move along now," Sergeant Watkins directed the onlookers.

The crowd parted as three more policemen arrived. They exchanged a few words with their fellow officer and then marched the prisoner off between them.

A few yards along the deck, the man turned round and, pulling at his handcuffed wrists, shouted at Josh, "I vill remember you. One day... one day..." and let out another stream of angry German. Josh looked a bit shaken.

"Officer," said Mrs. Hawkes-Lewis, who had by now rounded up the three girls, "will you please explain to me what this is all about? My son, it would seem, has assisted you greatly in apprehending a wanted criminal. What are you going to do about it?"

For all her severe exterior, she had a warmth about her which put Holly and Beth at their ease. Marjorie was holding her hand and had started to tell her excitedly how Peter had found the man and how he'd escaped over the fence, and she was beginning the story of their encounter with Gypsy Marigold when Sergeant Watkins interrupted.

"Yes indeed, ma'am, and I'm sure the force will show its gratitude. Firstly, though, I shall need to take down some details. Your name, young sir?"

"Josh Hawkes-Lewis. Well, it's Morris really, but Josh'll do. It wasn't just me, though. My friends here all helped."

"And your names?" He addressed the three girls and wrote carefully in his notepad. "Miss Marjorie Rowe..." So that was Marjorie's surname—Rowe. Holly and Beth looked at each other, both surprised that neither of them had known before. "Misses Holly and Elizabeth Randall. Perhaps you could all accompany me down to the station and..."

"No, no, officer. That is quite unnecessary." Mrs. Hawkes-Lewis was most insistent. "These young people have had a long day. You have their names, and here is my visiting card with our address. Should you need any more information, please call on me, and I shall arrange an interview for you with my son. Meanwhile, I am still waiting for an explanation."

Sergeant Watkins knew he was beaten. This formidable lady needed an answer, and he would try his best to give it.

It happened, he told Mrs. Hawkes-Lewis, that Josh was not the only one to have recognised Heinrich Muntz from the photograph in the newspaper. Several people out enjoying a Sunday afternoon stroll along the prom had spotted him, and his odd behaviour had soon aroused their suspicions. In the last hour, seven reports had been lodged at the police station, and two officers on the beat had been approached with news of possible sightings of him. The last report had come from a cyclist who had seen him enter the pier and who had immediately ridden at speed to the police station for help.

"And the rest, ma'am," said the policeman, "I believe you have heard from Miss Rowe here. If not, ma'am, I'm sure they'll be tellin' you all about it."

This seemed to satisfy Mrs. Hawkes-Lewis, at least for the time being. She thanked Sergeant Watkins and bid him good day, trusting that she would hear from him soon as to the outcome of the arrest and her son's courageous part in the capture of a wanted criminal and an enemy of the state, no less. Perhaps some recognition in the Police Gazette? With that, she turned and marched all four children and Peter off towards the pier entrance at a brisk pace, still holding on to her hat.

§ § § § §

Now they were back on the beach and the whole story had been related in great detail to Amelia, Dulcie, Tom and Bertie, Tallulah, her little sisters, and the still shaken Nurse May. The story lost nothing in the re-telling over and over again as questions were poured at the four heroes. Only when Josh broached upon the subject of Gypsy Marigold's strange visions in the crystal ball did Holly refuse to say anything and quickly changed the subject. In the excitement of the moment it was hardly noticed; there was so much else to tell.

"So," Mrs. Hawkes-Lewis addressed Holly and Beth, "might you young gels be Benaiah Randall's daughters? The blooms from his nursery are quite excellent, quite beautiful."

Beth was on the point of saying that their father's name was Stephen when, to her amazement, Holly replied, "Yes, and our mother's name is Maud. Father will be pleased to know you like his flowers; I'll tell him."

"Please do. And I should be pleased to welcome you all at my house for afternoon tea. Perhaps next Sunday would suit?"

"Er, well, that would be a bit difficult because we're going on holiday in a few days time. But it's very kind of you."

Benaiah Randall, of course! Beth remembered now what Holly had obviously already remembered. His name was on the oval wrought-iron sign that hung above the gates to the garden centre: 'Founded by Benaiah Randall, 1901.' It had been their centenary this year. He was their father's great-grandfather and his wife Maud's name had been on the card given out to customers with a brief history of the nurseries. Beth suddenly felt very proud of her family. That wrought iron sign was no longer just an old piece of metal with a funny name on it. Here she was actually talking to someone who had bought Benaiah's flowers and thought they were beautiful. The garden centre, which had always struck her as rather boring, would never be the same again.

§ § § § §

The wind had dropped and long streaks of high cloud trailed across the azure blue of the sky as they walked towards the beach hut. Katy would say it was a mackerel sky, an expression she'd learned from her mother. It always heralded fine weather.

Beth was deep in conversation with Marjorie, stopping every now and then to demonstrate the dance steps she'd been describing, holding Marjorie's hands to guide her. Their laughter rose into the clear air of the late afternoon.

Peter had taken a great liking to Holly and was trotting along at her heels, nudging against her every time they stopped. Holly picked up a pebble to throw for him, just a pale grey stone but with a broken line of rusty red running round it. It was warm from the spring sunshine, and her fingers felt the small indentations in its smooth surface. How funny that she should later remember such details of something as ordinary as a pebble.

A little way along, Marjorie spotted a bench, well positioned for a view over the low sea wall.

"Let's sit down and pretend we're the old ladies who come here for the afternoon to do their knitting and look at the sea," she said. "I'm just learning to knit. I'm knitting a scarf for a soldier at the Front. It's purple. Dulcie's is much nicer, though. Hers is red and much thicker, and her knitting needles are much fatter. I don't know why Mother bought me such thin needles; it'll take me ages longer to finish my scarf."

They all sat in a row, with Peter at their feet. Holly had been anxious to get back to the beach hut after her strange vision on the pier, but now she felt she wanted the afternoon to last forever.

"Do you know who you're knitting the scarf for?" asked Beth. "I mean, do you know anyone who's fighting in the war now?"

"They're not usually for anyone in particular. We just knit lots of things at school and Miss Tyler—she's our headmistress—sends them out. Daddy's not allowed to join up because he works for the Government," she said, "but he's joined something called Territorials. Is your father fighting in the war?"

Holly said, "Well, er... no, because, because we grow vegetables and things as well as flowers and it's important because everyone needs food."

She'd suddenly remembered something else she'd read in the leaflet on the history of Benaiah Randall's nursery garden: during both the World Wars part of the land had been given over to food production. What a stroke of luck that the memory should come to her just then.

"Oh, I see." Marjorie seemed to accept it without question. "You must be very pleased he's not out in France or Belgium. One of the girls at school—she's called Doris—has got a brother who's at the Front and she's knitting a scarf for him. He was fighting at Mons last year, and he *saw the angel!* Doris told us all about it; she brought his letter to school at the beginning of the autumn term. Lots of his friends were killed, so he was lucky. Do you believe in angels?"

"Yes, definitely," Beth said. Holly nodded in agreement.

"So do I. Would you like a humbug?" She took a little twist of brown paper from her pocket. "I think they're lovely."

Holly burst out laughing. Marjorie was just like Josh—all serious one minute, then lighthearted and jolly the next. The humbugs were very sticky and for a few moments none of them spoke.

Then Marjorie said, "I know! Beth and I will put on a show for you, Holly. Come on, Beth, we'll do the dance together, the one you just taught me. Holly, you've got to clap and cheer and pretend you're a big crowd of people at the Balham Assembly Rooms. Shall we do that, Beth? Come on."

So Holly moved off the bench and sat on the sea wall to watch while Marjorie and Beth joined hands and bowed low together. Somewhere in the distance, a barrel organ was playing. With just a few hesitations and promptings from Beth, Marjorie was soon dancing alongside her in the steps she'd been shown, following the rhythm of the distant music. Their steps became faster and faster, the little girl from 1915 in her knitted wool coat and the little girl from 2001 in her brightly coloured sarong, and then Peter was up on his hind legs, joining in too. Holly cheered them on, clapping and laughing, until all at once they collapsed in a fit of giggles.

"Mother would be so cross if she could see me now," Marjorie said, between fits of laughter. "She'd say... she'd say I look as if I'd been 'dragged up in the gutter.' It's one of Mother's expressions." More giggles, then, feeling she was being disloyal, Marjorie added, "But you'll like Mother when you get to know her; she's lovely. I wish you weren't going away so soon. We've got to move away from London. Daddy's got a new job in Wales, the Government asked him to go. I know!" She brightened up. "You could come to stay with us when we've moved to our new house. I'll ask Mother to write to your mother and arrange it. That's what we'll do. You would come, wouldn't you?"

Holly, feeling almost overwhelmingly sad, said, "We'd love to, but you see, we may be a long, long way away. We're going on holiday very soon and then, well—"

"We don't really know what's happening," said Beth. "Daddy hasn't told us yet."

"Yes, but we can write, and you won't be away for ever and ever, will you? Will you give me your address? Then as soon as I know our new one, I'll write to you. I know I'll see you again. I know, know, know I will. Maybe we'll all be very old ladies by then, but we will see each other again."

Beth was trying to push away the memory of that quiet bungalow where, until so recently, Mrs. Hawkes-Lewis, Amelia, had lived. It was all so unreal, so impossible.

Then Marjorie started to giggle again as she sat on the bench pretending to be a very old lady with her knitting.

After a moment she said, "I've got an idea! You could *all* come on holiday to Wales. I love holidays. Mother starts packing ages and ages beforehand. It's so exciting seeing the trunk all ready to go off and then Mother puts the 'P' or 'CP' card in the window for the carrier so he'll come and pick it up. I love seeing the card up, don't you? Then you know your holiday's almost starting."

"What's 'P' and 'CP'?" asked Holly. "Don't you take your luggage with you?"

"Of course not, it would be far too heavy!" Marjorie gave Holly a look of amazement. "Don't you have carriers in Brighton? I thought everyone had them. Perhaps it's only in London then. Well, 'P' is for Pickford's and 'CP' is for Carter-Paterson's. It's called Passenger Luggage in Advance. Then when you get to your boarding house, it's there ready for you. Once I told Peter that if he wasn't good, I'd send him in advance, too!" Marjorie leaned down and patted the little fox terrier's head. "But he knew I didn't mean it. Couldn't you come back here tomorrow? Oh no, silly me, I'll be at school. We've got to go home tonight."

"Marjorie! It's time to go."

Mrs. Rowe was calling to her, hurrying towards them along the prom. Their afternoon together was all too suddenly drawing to a close.

"Golly, I'd better hurry! We've got to catch the train." Marjorie leaned down to fasten some buttons on her boot that had come undone while she'd been dancing. "Please tell me your address so I can write to you. I haven't got anything to write on, so I'll have to remember it."

"Okay," said Beth, ignoring Holly's warning glance. "It's 27, Nightingale Road, Brighton, East Sussex, BN1…" Holly was shaking her head furiously at Beth.

Before she could continue, Marjorie said, "What's BN1 mean? Josh doesn't have letters and numbers after his address. And why do you call it East Sussex? It's just Sussex. I've written it lots of time."

"BN1's the postcode, but don't worry about it because—" Holly began.

"Oh, it's like we have in London. We used to be just SW, but now we're SW17. We live at 53, Arthur Road, London, South West Seventeen," she said, pronouncing the postal district very carefully. "I'd better hurry properly now; Mother's calling me again, and there's Dulcie waving to us, too. Please, please write back. You will, won't you? I'll send you my address in Wales." Marjorie was walking and skipping backwards down the prom towards her mother with Peter at her heels.

"It might be difficult," called out Beth, adding, to Holly's horror, "because you see we come from the future. We come from 2001. We came here through the beach hut and—"

"And I came from 1066 through the bandstand! You do say such funny things." Marjorie was almost out of earshot now, but there was laughter in her voice. "*Au revoir! A bientot!* Twenty-seven, Nightingale Road... Twenty-seven, Nightingale Road... it's in my brain now."

She turned round to run the last few yards and then, just as she reached her mother and Dulcie, she called out, "Oh, I forgot to tell you! Mother's got your—"

But the wind took away her final words.

15

The three distant figures were all waving now, Marjorie with both hands high above her head and jumping up and down in her eagerness to be seen. But they looked just a little hazy; perhaps it was the brightness reflected off the sparkling sea.

Holly and Beth waved and waved until their friends had disappeared from view farther down the prom. The day was still so bright, although it was late in the afternoon. There was not a cloud in the sky, but somewhere high above them, a yellow dot was growing gradually bigger. Then they spotted that the dot had a tail, and soon the shape became quite clear.

The yellow balloon they'd taken such pains to rescue and which had led them into such an adventure swooped towards them on a gust of wind. They tried to catch the string, but just as Holly had it, another gust tore it from her hand and sent it flying out to sea.

"It's gone!" shouted Beth as she ran back up the stony beach after her vain attempt to catch up with the balloon. They had reached the beach hut now, and she sat down out of breath on the wooden step.

"It's gone, just like our adventure. It's flown away like Marjorie and all her friends. They've all gone. We'll never see them again, will we? You don't think we'll ever get back again, do you?" she said, almost angrily. "It's not fair. I've decided. I'm not going in. Once we shut those doors, we'll never get back again, will we?"

Holly had opened the beach hut doors, but sat down on the step next to Beth. She said nothing, but shielded her eyes against the sun, watching the yellow balloon as it drifted farther and farther out of

sight. She wanted to take in every detail of what they could see. There
was the West Pier with its flags flying and the beautiful new concert
hall in the making; she especially wanted to remember that. She
wanted to be able to think about it every time she looked at the poor,
ruined shell of the once grand building. And there were the people in
their Sunday best coming and going, though not so many now, and
still the sound of the barrel organ playing somewhere in the distance.
It was almost like theme music to a film she was watching, although
she wasn't watching it, she was in it.

She stood up and looked back towards the town, for she wanted to
remember the buildings she could see from the prom, the hotels she
recognised from her own time and others long gone. There were the
Metropole and The Grand, that she knew so well, but farther along
was Allen's Boarding House, that she definitely didn't recognise.
What was in its place? She couldn't think. Next to it was a stone arch-
way and over it a dark green painted sign with letters in gold which
read 'Apollo Harness Maker.' It looked curiously out of place on the
seafront.

Her gaze was drawn back to the beach where some fishing boats
and dinghies were pulled up on the shingle near the West Pier. An old
man in a faded, navy blue jumper was painting with thick black tar
the bottom of a dinghy that lay upside down on the stones next to a
fishing boat called Golden Promise. He must have spotted Holly as
she looked at him, for he gave her a little wave. She noticed there
were specks of tar in his rather long, grey beard; yet how could she?
Surely, he was far too far away for her to see such detail?

Even as she tried to take in all that she could see around her, she
was thinking about Marjorie's hastily shouted message: *"Mother's
got your—"* What was it? What could her mother have? She sat down
again on the beach hut step and stared out to sea.

Beth seemed to be reading her thoughts.

"What d'you think Marjorie meant when she said her mother had
got your 'something'?" she said. "What happened when you came
here without me?"

"I don't know," said Holly, "I just can't think. It's really stupid;
there's something really important I'm forgetting, but I can't think
what it is. Come on, we've got to go back, you know we have. We
can't just sit here until it gets dark. Anyway, Marjorie and the others
have all gone now, and it's because of them that we're here, I'm sure.
Because of Marjorie, anyway. Come on."

She stepped inside and Beth grudgingly followed. They shut the doors behind them and sat down on the benches in silence. But not for long.

"Of course!" Holly suddenly remembered. "The photo! The one I told you about of me with the monkey and the lady I recognised in the museum photo. I never collected it—I couldn't because we came back nearly a year later. If only I'd got it, that would prove everything." Holly looked devastated.

"D'you think Marjorie's mother could have got it? How could she, though?" Beth had brightened up a little.

"Because the photographer was going to hang it up by his stand with all his other photos ready for collection. Mrs. Rowe could've recognised me and got it for me. And now I'll never, ever get it."

Holly leaned back against the wooden wall of the beach hut, biting her lip and trying desperately not to cry. Beth felt sorry for her. She came over to sit next to Holly and, very uncharacteristically, put her arm round her neck.

"You never know, maybe you will. Mrs. Rowe might have sent it to you and..."

"Yes, but she would have sent it eighty-six years ago! We don't even know who was living in our house then. It would have been almost new—what a funny thought. And anyway, whoever was, wouldn't have known who I was, so they would have thrown it away. No, it's lost forever."

"We mustn't give up. There may still be a way. We could ask Mr. Edwards! He might have an idea." Beth was pleased with her moment of inspiration.

"I suppose we could. He might be able to find out who lived in our house in 1915. I suppose we could try." They lapsed into silence again.

But someone was knocking on the door. They could hear people outside, talking, laughing, and shouting. The knob gradually turned and Jessica's mother, Jenny, put her head round the door.

"You two must be so hot in there. Why have you got the doors shut? It's beautiful out here."

The shock was almost too much to take as the noise and bustle of the twenty-first century burst in upon them. Old Rollo next door started barking as a skateboarder steered dangerously near him. Groups of small children played noisily by the sea wall and, down on the beach, Jamie was blowing his whistle, trying to keep control of some boys fighting each other in the shallows.

Holly and Beth felt dazed. What had been happening before they left all those hours ago for that quieter but happy time on the beach in 1915? It was all a bit of a blur.

"What's up with you two?" laughed Jenny. "You look as if you've seen a ghost. And why ever are you wearing your fleeces? You must be boiled."

"Oh, we got a bit cold after swimming." Holly hastily pulled off her fleece.

"Hang on," said Jenny, "you said you wouldn't go in again while I was away. What's been going on?"

"No, we didn't," said Beth. "We just got cold from the first time. Where's Jess?"

"Sorry, but you both looked awfully as if you had a guilty secret. Are you sure there's nothing going on?" Jenny was unconvinced as they shook their heads but decided it was best to change the subject for the time being. "Well then, I've left Jess at the cafe having an ice cream and resting her foot. Would you like to join her?"

On the way to the cafe, Jenny told the girls how lucky they'd been at the First Aid station. They hadn't had to wait at all and the St. John's Ambulance officers on duty had been wonderful. They soon had Jess's foot cleaned, inspected for glass particles—a few of which they had found and carefully removed—and comfortably bandaged. They commended Jamie, she said, on his first aid and Jess on her bravery. What a blessing it was to have a service like that so close to the beach.

When they arrived at the cafe, Jessica was looking much better. The colour had returned to her face completely. She had her bandaged foot up on a chair and was licking a strawberry ice cream.

"Hi!" she said, "Are you getting ice creams, too? I thought they were only for people with *serious injuries.*" She stressed the last two words dramatically.

Holly had a chocolate chip ice cream, and Beth chose a mango and pineapple one.

"When you've finished those, we'd better be getting back for our picnic," said Jenny. "The ice creams are by way of recovery from shock. I don't know what your Mum would say to ice creams before sandwiches."

"Oh, she wouldn't mind," said Beth. "Anyway, Holly and I had ours before we went to—"

"Before you went where? I knew there was something going on!" Jenny looked triumphant. "I've caught you out now."

"Before we went to talk to Maureen and Rollo," Holly said. "The sandwiches were very nice. Thank you very much for the lunch."

"Right, I see." Jenny shook her head and smiled. "Anyway, you're both all right, that's the main thing."

After lunch—Holly and Beth found they could manage another sandwich each—Jenny suggested that Jessica should rest at the beach hut in a deck chair rather than try to negotiate the crowds on the beach with her injured foot. She had a book to read, and it was always fun just watching the people on the prom. To Jessica's annoyance, Jenny insisted she wore her sunhat and applied more sun cream, for the sun was bright and hot. She herself had some letters to write, so would keep Jess company and supply drinks when needed. That way, the foot would soon recover.

"You two can go on the beach again now if you like," said Jenny, "but promise to come and tell me if you're going for another swim, and tell Jamie so that he can look out for you."

"We don't need to do that," said Beth. "Mummy always lets us—"

"Okay, we promise," said Holly. "But can we tell you now that we're going for a swim? We'll tell Jamie, really we will. Come on, Beth." Holly had learned that it saved a lot of time to agree with grown-ups, especially when it was something not too troublesome. Beth glared at her, but didn't argue.

"All right, but don't go out too far," said Jenny. "You've only just had that other sandwich."

§ § § § §

The beach was more crowded than ever. A lot of people were dozing after their picnic lunches, lying on towels or sprawled in deck chairs with hats over their faces. A crowd of small children, watched by their mothers or fathers, were playing at the sea's edge where the tide had uncovered a small strip of sand below the pebbles, but there was hardly anyone in the sea.

Jamie was sitting in a deck chair inside the rescue boat, officially scanning the sea for possible trouble, but half reading 'Hello' magazine and dozing. He jumped when Holly spoke to him.

"Oh, hi there, kids. Yes, sure I'll keep an eye on you. It'll be dead easy to spot you at the moment; everyone's on siesta."

"Thanks, Jamie," said Holly.

They started off towards the sea, leaving their towels and flip-flops by the boat as usual, when Jamie called out to them.

"Hey, wait a sec, kids! Have you got your friend with you? I'd better look out for her too if she's going in with you."

"No, she's resting her foot." Holly looked amazed. How could Jamie think that Jessica could be going swimming? He was the one who'd come to her rescue after the accident.

"No, not Jessica!" Jamie laughed. "I'd be telling her off good and proper if she tried to swim this afternoon. No, the friend who was on the old pier with you just now. Come to think of it, how'd you get back here so quickly? And how were you allowed on without an adult? They're right fussy with the guided tours. You must've been cheeky to talk your way on."

The girls stopped dead in their tracks. Beth made a kind of gasp. A shiver ran down Holly's spine. What was Jamie saying? Could he really have seen them?

"You saw us?" she said, "You saw *three* of us on the pier together? But how?"

"Ah well, that's the point, isn't it? I was out in the rescue boat 'cos some silly girl had gone out too far in her inflatable and the wind caught it and was taking her out to sea. Her dad tried to swim after her, but her mum—a sensible woman—got me. By the time I reached the girl, her dad needed rescuing, too. He was fat, and I mean FAT!" Jamie indicated the man's size with his arms. "He'd tired himself out. I saw you on the pier, leaning on the railings. I called out to you and waved. I was quite near; you must have seen me."

Then it came back to Holly, that odd moment when she was so sure someone was watching them. And she'd been sure it was someone from the sea. So she was right; it wasn't her imagination. Jamie had seen them although they couldn't see him. But how could he have done? Could it have been in the same way she had suddenly, just for a second, seen the old pier in 1915? Was it the vanishing point in time again, the parallel lines coming together?

A great surge of excitement welled up in her. But why should Jamie have seen them? And old Mr. Jim, he'd seen Marjorie go into the beach hut with Peter. No one else had seen her. What was special about Jamie and his grandpa?

"You really saw us? All three of us? But there was someone else with us, our friend's cousin. He's fifteen and quite tall—didn't you see him?"

"No, just you two and the other girl. For a moment, I thought I saw a dog, but I must have imagined it; dogs aren't allowed on the old pier. I called out to you quite loudly and gave you a wave. Oh, I get it!" Jamie laughed. "You hadn't told Jess's mum you were going and you weren't meant to be there. You didn't want me to see you, did you? But how on earth did you get there and back so quickly? Beats me."

"You wouldn't want to know," said Holly.

"And you wouldn't believe us if we told you," added Beth. "Can we go for a swim now?"

"Okay, in a minute. But go on, try me. Try and see if I believe you."

Beth glanced at Holly, but she was staring out to sea in the direction of the old pier.

"Okay then," she said. "When you saw us, it wasn't now, in 2001. It was in 1915. We got there through the beach hut. We closed the doors, and when we opened them again we were in 1915. We've done it before, but it was 1914 then. But when we're there, the time stays the same here. Well, almost the same. So that's how we got back so quickly. It's really cool being in 1915, and our friends there are really cool, too. The First World War's on and we heard lots about it. Some of it was very sad, but we had a *great* adventure. We were on the pier and…"

"Oh, go off with you! Have your swim." Jamie laughed. "I used to make up stories like that when I was a kid."

"But it's not made up, we really did—"

"Don't bother, Beth." Holly turned back from staring at the old pier; it looked so forlorn and sad even on this bright day. "Jamie'll never believe us. No one will."

Mr. Edwards had told Holly they should talk about what had happened to them and their travels into the past. But what was the point? No one was going to believe them, not even Jamie, who was the only person who'd actually seen Marjorie with them.

"Okay then, we're going swimming now. Just Holly and me," said Beth.

"I'll watch out for you." Jamie grinned and settled back in his deck chair. But he was puzzled.

Maybe he'd talk to Gramps about it.

16

That night, Beth shared Holly's bedroom, sleeping on the futon bed next to the big sash window. She'd asked her mother if she might do this because Holly's room was bigger and airier than hers, and the night was so warm. But the real reason was that she didn't want to be alone. There was too much to talk about, too much was going through her brain for her to sleep.

Lying in their beds they could see the vast canopy of stars, a view interrupted only by the branches of the apple tree just over on the right, silhouetted against the darkening sky. It was easy in this light to imagine they could be back in Marjorie's time. There was no sound of a car engine or even a plane, just the soft night-time song of birds settling down to rest and the creaking of the old house as it, too, rested from the heat of the day.

Beth kicked off her duvet and turned her pillow over for the third time.

"It's no good," she said, "I knew it wouldn't be. I'm not going to even try to sleep. It's hot, and I don't feel even the littlest bit tired. I keep thinking about…well, everything. Marjorie and Peter, the German spy, all that stuff about the war. And I don't want to forget it." She yawned in spite of herself. "You know what it's like with dreams sometimes? You have this brilliant dream, and it's like it's real, and then when you wake up you think you'll remember it forever. But then a bit later, you can remember it hardly at all, at least not the exciting bits, and then it's gone forever. It would be awful if that happened and then we'll start to think we just imagined everything."

"No, we won't," insisted Holly, "because we were both there together. Well, most of the time anyway. I wish so much you'd been there every time. I might start thinking I'd imagined the time when I was there without you, 'specially as I haven't got the photo. Oh, if only I'd been able to get that photo!" Holly tossed her duvet onto the floor and clicked on her bedside light. "Just to make sure," she said, "let's write down everything we can remember. Here, come and get a pencil and some paper."

Beth sat down on the bed next to Holly and for a while they wrote fast and in silence, punctuated only by questions to jog each other's memories on small details.

"You know," Holly said after she'd filled three pages of A4 with hastily scribbled writing, "I just wish so much that Granny and Grandpa were here, and we could tell them about everything. They'd understand, I know they would. Or even Great-Granny. She might even have been alive in 1914."

"But Great-Granny's too ill. And anyway, she can't talk, can she, since she had the...the..."

"Stroke. She had a stroke, Mummy said. Mummy was very sad. She said Great-Granny might not even know us anymore. Anyway, I don't think she could be that old. But when Granny and Grandpa come back from Canada, we could tell them. Aunty Rachel must have her baby soon."

"Mummy said it was supposed to have been born last week. Are you going to put in the bit about Gypsy Marigold? It must have been really scary." Beth pushed back a lock of hair that had fallen over her face and continued writing.

"That's what Josh does!" Holly laughed. "He pushes back his hair just like that. Or, well, he did. I don't know whether we can talk about him in the present or the past. I can't possibly think of Marjorie as being just in the past, can you?"

"Not possibly. She's not anyway. What was the German spy's name? Henry something, wasn't it?"

For several minutes more the girls sat side-by-side, writing away furiously, now and then comparing notes and correcting each other. An owl hooted somewhere in the distance, and the light from a car's headlamps reflected on the edge of the bedroom wall nearest the window. They heard a door slam and the crunch of gravel on the short drive.

"Daddy's home," said Holly. "He was working late 'cos we're going on holiday. I wonder if, oh well, I suppose it doesn't matter now."

"You wonder what?" asked Beth. Although insisting that she couldn't sleep a wink, her eyes were tiring. She picked up all her written sheets, carefully checking that they were in the right order, and then put down her pencil. "What do you wonder? I think I'll have to stop now."

"Well, if we hadn't been going on holiday," said Holly, "would we have had another chance to go back again? It was almost as if Marjorie was leaving *because* we were going on holiday. I know that doesn't seem to make sense, but if it was meant to happen, would we have met them all at some different time if we weren't going away?" Holly folded her sheets of paper and put them under her pillow. "I mean, it looks as if it happened like it did so that we wouldn't miss each other. So that we wouldn't go back to 1914 or 1915 or whenever and not find Marjorie, if you see what I mean."

"Sort of," said Beth with a big yawn. "But actually no, I don't know what you're talking about." She lay down on Holly's bed and in the next few seconds was fast asleep.

"Beth, you're in my bed! I need to…oh well, you stay there."

Holly went over to the futon and lay down, too. She was determined to stay awake, to try to relive every moment of their extraordinary adventures and set them firmly in her memory, but her eyelids became heavy. She'd close her eyes, she thought, just for a moment, to rest them. Then, at that strange point between wakefulness and sleep when everything can seem a little fantastical, she imagined she was in the beach hut again, on her own and holding the note from Marjorie. There it was in her hand: Holly and Beth, The Beach Hut, Brighton, England, Europe, The World, The Universe. There was Marjorie's neat writing, just as she had seen it before. She would have to go and look for Beth, for they must be sure to go together. But she was so tired; maybe it could wait just a little while.

Holly fell into a deep, dreamless sleep.

§ § § § §

Jamie spent a lot of time at his grandfather's house. During term time at the university, he lived with old Jim. It saved him money, for student accommodation in Brighton was not cheap, and his grandfather enjoyed his company. In fact, they both enjoyed each other's company. Jamie's parents lived in Sheffield; the family had moved there from Hove, just down the road from Brighton, when his father's office had been relocated.

Jim had missed them sorely, and Jamie's presence in the little house on the beach had breathed new life into him. He took pride in sending his grandson off with a good cooked breakfast inside him before he cycled to the university every morning. This year, Jamie had asked if he could stay on for the summer holidays; the job of lifeguard had a touch of glamour about it, he could indulge his favourite sport of swimming, and the pay wasn't bad either.

Sometimes Jamie would invite his university friends over and they'd have a barbecue on the beach. Jim would take his fishing rod and a little lantern down to the sea's edge and sit on the shingle contentedly as he listened to their chatter and music. It made him feel young again.

Jim had bought the house on the beach fifty-five years before on what was then the unfashionable end and property was cheap, long before pop stars and the like started buying up the houses there. He and his beloved wife, Lily, had spent the best years of their life in the house, a life watched over by the rise and fall of the tide, the coming and going of migrating birds and always the sound of the waves almost on their doorstep. It had hardly changed in all that time, and when Lily died two years back, he never wanted to change it. Jamie, too, seemed happy to leave things as they'd always been. He'd touch up the paintwork when it was needed, gather driftwood for the wood-burning stove in the sitting room, and the old Raeburn stove kept the kitchen cosy all the year round.

On this warm summer night, they both sat outside on the little veranda, Jim in his favourite green and white striped deck chair, which was faded by the sun, and Jamie beside him in a weatherworn wicker chair with a high back. On the far horizon, the lights of a big ship glowed in the deep blue of the sea and a sky that was streaked with the golden embers of the setting sun. The old West Pier stood out starkly, a black silhouette against the blue, but away in the distance to the east the Palace Pier dazzled the skyline, ablaze with dancing lights that moved and shimmered in the gathering darkness. On the beach below them, a few late waders could still be seen at the water's edge, little birds, not much bigger than blackbirds, whose sweet evening song heralded the approaching night. Hardly a ripple disturbed the surface of the sea.

The old man and the young man sat in companionable silence. They'd had a good supper and enjoyed a glass of beer together. Jim lit up his pipe, a habit of so many years that he reckoned he'd be hard pushed to give it up now. The tobacco glowed red in the bowl of the pipe as he drew on the stem. He settled back comfortably, watching the smoke drift into the warm night.

Jamie had an enamel mug of coffee on the veranda beside his chair. He picked it up and put it down again.

"Gramps, you know the Randall kids?"

"Miss Holly and Miss Beth? Nice young kiddies. Well mannered. Did you see them today?" Jim closed his eyes. Jamie wasn't sure if he was going off to sleep.

"They were on the beach most of the day, just below their beach hut where I keep the rescue boat. Their friend cut her foot badly on some broken glass. I gave her first aid and sent her and her mum off to the St. John's Ambulance place."

"She all right then?" Jim puffed on his pipe again.

"She was fine. Bit shaken, but we got her fixed up."

"Good lad. You keep at it."

"Yes, but a funny thing happened," said Jamie. "Just after, I had to go out in the boat on a rescue—usual story, kid adrift on an inflatable gone out too far on a falling tide—"

"You got her? Good lad. You do a grand job." Jim still had his eyes closed but was listening attentively to his grandson.

"Yes, I got her, and her dad. Right near the old pier. That was the funny thing, though. I happened to look up at the old pier, and I spotted Holly and Beth and another young girl leaning on the rail. I waved to them, but they didn't seem to see me."

"They must have moved like the clappers! Thought you said they was on the beach near you. Sure it was them?"

"Definitely," said Jamie. "But then I saw them back on the beach again. They couldn't've done it. Not there and back in that time."

"Did you tell 'em you'd seen 'em? What did they say?" Jim had opened his eyes and was pulling himself into an upright position in the old deck chair.

"It was Beth, the younger one. I think she was playing a game with me. Kids like playing these fanciful games, don't they? She said...oh, I don't know why I'm bothered about it really; it was only a game. But she said..." Jamie paused, staring out to sea.

"What did she say then?" Jim waited. A dog barked somewhere along the shore, followed by the sound of a woman's voice calling to it.

"She said—you're going to laugh when you hear this—she said they'd been on the pier with a friend, but that is was in 1915, not 2001. She said they'd gone through the beach hut and found themselves there." Jamie gave a small laugh. "What stories kids make up, I ask you! She said it dead seriously, too."

"What makes you think she made it up? They're good kiddies, not given to storytelling. I've known 'em since they was not much more than babbies." Jim tapped the bowl of his pipe and drew in some more air to ignite the tobacco again.

"Come on, Gramps! What're you saying? That they really did go, well, time-travelling through the beach hut?" Jamie didn't laugh this time; his curiosity was getting the better of him.

"Reckon so," said Jim. "I've had my suspicions afore. Remember I told you about a young lass going into the beach hut along wi' a dog? She was dressed kinda funny. Then when we 'ad all that rain a couple 'o weeks back, I found the Randall hut open and small sandy foot-marks on the floor inside. And there was this little belt on the floor, white with a kind 'o buckle to it. I hung it up, but it'd disappeared when Miss Holly and her mum came along. Reckon it was the kiddy from them far-off times that'd been there."

"Gramps, this is crazy! You're saying it could actually happen? But why? How? Or do you mean that this other girl was a ghost?" Jamie couldn't believe what he was hearing.

"Ghost? No, no ghost. Must've 'appened like Miss Beth said." Jim tapped the bowl of his pipe again and puffed a little more smoke into the air.

"But Gramps, this is crazy!" Jamie repeated. "People can't just, well, go back in time. It sounds like some kind of sci-fi story or—"

"No, nothing like that, young Jim." Gramps was the only one who called Jamie by that name, but he liked it from the old man. "I don't believe ordinary folk'd be able to do it," Jim continued, "but kiddies can. You see, their brains aren't crowded out wi' knowing too many things and too much reasoning. Their brains is not telling 'em some-thing can't 'appen because it ain't possible, so things can 'appen that to us older folks, with all our reasoning and so on, don't seem possi-ble. That's how I looks at it."

"Then why should you and I have seen this young kid? She looked pretty normal to me, except that…well, she was wearing a sort of coat and hat which did seem a bit odd, now I come to think of it. It was far too hot for coats, even out on the pier. Oh, this is ridiculous! Now I'm beginning to talk like you." Jamie laughed.

"That's my lad. You just keep an open mind while we both thinks about it. Most folks aren't good at that. Now, maybe—and I'm not saying it is or it isn't—but maybe, if they *was* back in 1915, it wasn't 'ot and it wasn't summer. Did you ask Miss Beth?"

"Are you joking? I just laughed at the story. Holly said something like 'nobody'll ever believe us,' but I thought she was kidding, too." Jamie paused, waiting for a reaction from Jim, but he seemed lost in thought. "Okay, so why the beach hut, then? What's special about that?"

For a moment, the old man said nothing. The stars seemed brighter than ever in the deepening blue of the sky, but the big tanker they'd seen so ablaze with lights on the horizon had now disappeared. The stillness was broken only by the gentle lap of the waves on the shore and the distant sound of laughter from along the beach where they could just see the glow from a campfire.

He didn't answer Jamie's question at first. "You see that big tanker out there on the horizon?" he said.

"No, I can't see it at all now. You must've got better sight than me if you can see it, Gramps. But what about…"

"But it don't mean it ain't there any more just because we can't see it no more, do it, lad?" Jim smiled at his grandson and patted his arm. "And what about them stars? We can see 'em, but some o' them ain't there no more, so those scientist chappies tell us. What was you asking me, son?"

"About the beach hut. Why should it be a sort of door into the past, if what you're saying could possibly be true? What so special about beach huts?"

Jamie's mind was working overtime. Why was he asking these questions? He couldn't really believe what his grandfather was telling him. Could he?

"Ah, well, now you're talking. Beach 'uts *is* special. They've been there for a long time. Not necessarily the same ones, oh no. They get blown down, or washed away, or just damaged wi' time and the sea air. But they don't change, do beach 'uts." Jim leaned forward and knocked some ash from his pipe onto the shingle in front of the veranda. "They 'ave some different things inside of 'em according to the times, like, but they don't really change. An' folks is 'appy in 'em. Folks 'ave always been 'appy in 'em. 'Appiness gets into 'em and sticks around—bit like this place, really. So there ain't no barrier, like. I've been looking after beach 'uts for a long time, and now and then I sees things."

"Okay, but you haven't answered my other question. Why us? Why you and me?"

Jamie was sure that in the cold light of day he'd never be asking such things. But the night was so still and the stars so dazzling that, just at this moment, he felt he could believe anything.

"Didn't I? Well, I reckon it's like this. If I sees something a bit strange, like them little sandy footprints, I says to meself 'what's going on 'ere?' and I thinks about it a bit. But the beach and I—and the sea—we're old friends. We've been together a long time; we got to know each other. I don't say to the sea 'why does you come and go like that? Why does you move them stones around and change the shape 'o the beach from time to time?' Yes, I knows it's the moon and all that, but I don't go reasoning a lot. The Good Lord made it like that, so it's all right by me. I don't want to know no scientific explanations. So maybe He gave me this gift to see like kiddies do. Reckon you must've got it off 'o me, for all your college learning."

Jim laughed softly and shifted a little in his deck chair. "Now, how about a nice cup o' tea for your old granddad?"

Even in the summer, Jim kept the Raeburn going. A few minutes later, Jamie handed his grandfather a mug of tea, well sugared and stirred, just as he liked it. The peace of the night surrounded them as they watched the last golden rays on the horizon sink into the sea.

"Tell you what, sonny," it was old Jim who broke the silence, "I wish I could've done it. They're blessed, they are, those kiddies. Real blessed."

17

"But he can't be! We really, really need to see him."

Holly couldn't believe what Miss Jones was saying. She wouldn't believe it; how could Mr. Edwards be away now? It was just too unfair.

Miss Jones sighed. She'd had a busy morning and already several requests from visitors to the museum to see Mr. Edwards. She wished she were going away, too; school holidays could be very trying, what with extra activities going on almost every day and children running around where they shouldn't be. It was all too much.

"Well, I'm sorry," she said, very firmly, "but I'm afraid he *is* on holiday. He and his wife are touring Andalucia for two weeks. They left this afternoon." She turned back to her computer screen, shuffled a few papers, and hoped that Holly and Beth would go away.

"*Two weeks?* It's going to be too late." Beth looked quite angry. "You see it's…"

"Look, girls, I'm sorry, but Mr. Edwards really is not here. Why don't you go and have a look round upstairs? We've got some new exhibits in the costume gallery." Miss Jones softened her tone a little. Maybe she was being a bit harsh; Mr. Edwards, she knew, would not like it.

"Thank you, we might do that. Come on, Beth." Holly shut the office door behind them, feeling very dispirited.

They had woken to grey skies and a fine drizzle. The hot, sunny world of the day before had vanished with the dawn. Katy had been hurrying around in a minor panic, retrieving dirty washing from their bedrooms, all of which had to be laundered and ready to pack by the next day. Breakfast had been against a background of Katy's frustration with the weather and the impossibility of getting anything dried and aired in time. Then Mrs. Dawson from next door had called to say that she couldn't feed the cat after all because her sister was ill and she had to go up to Nottingham to look after her. Stephen had left late, to his annoyance, after making frantic phone calls to organise replacement temporary staff now that his two best workers had called in sick.

Holly and Beth were only too pleased when Katy suggested that, if they couldn't do anything useful, maybe they'd like to catch the bus into town and pick up some shopping for her.

They'd rushed through the list as quickly as possible in order to have time to spend at the museum. They needed Mr. Edwards's help; no one else would know what to do, and besides, they had so much they wanted to tell him. And now here they were, their hopes dashed. They were leaving for France the day after tomorrow and were no nearer to finding out who Marjorie Rowe was and why she'd come into their lives.

"Oh, come on, we might as well have a look around while we're here," said Holly. "We don't want to go back to the madhouse just yet. We'll leave the shopping in the cloakroom."

Somewhat dejectedly, they walked up the old stone staircase to the first floor. It was silly really; here they were about to go off on a foreign holiday for the first time in their lives and yet their enthusiasm at that moment could not have been less.

Soon, they were in the gallery where Holly had spent so long before staring at the figures of the mother and daughter as they stood in the parlour where the bells were so prominently displayed. But now there was a doll's pram in the room as well, a beautiful little coach-built pram on an elegant metal chassis. It had two small wheels at the front and two large wheels at the back, and a curved metal handle with an ivory grip. A doll was tucked up under a pretty satin cover with a pleated edge.

Beth stood stock still, staring through the glass protecting the exhibits.

"That's Jack!" she said.

"Jack who?" said Holly, trying to see where Beth was looking. "There's no one else in here. What're you talking about?"

"The doll, stupid. It's Jack, I know it is. Marjorie told me about him. I specially remember because he's a boy doll, and you don't often have boy dolls."

The doll was half leaning, half seated in the pram and he—for surely it was a he—wore a little sailor shirt with a square collar edged in navy blue and a perfect replica of a sailor's hat over his golden curls. His rosebud mouth was painted in a slight smile, and he had thick lashes over his blue glass eyes.

"He's a bit girly," said Holly, "but it's a cool hat he's wearing. How d'you know it's Jack, though? There were probably hundreds and thousands of dolls made like that. You can't possibly be sure."

"He was made in Germany, Marjorie told me," said Beth, her face pressed to the glass. "She said she couldn't let on because people hate everything German. They even hate dachshunds because they're German sausage dogs. I mean, well, they did then. But she really, really loved Jack. I wish I could go in and pick him up."

"But you still can't be sure." Holly was unconvinced.

"It's Jack." Beth spoke with perfect conviction. A thousand arguments would not have dissuaded her at that moment.

It was very quiet in the gallery; maybe all the children who had so annoyed Miss Jones earlier had gone to have lunch. Now the only sound from inside was the gentle ticking of the grandfather clock in the entrance hall as it measured the seconds, just as it had done for the last one hundred and fifty-seven years. There is something special about the tick of a grandfather clock, a kind of confidence in the tone that suggests time will go on, just so, unhurried, unaffected by the bustle and noise of the ever-changing modern world. You can hear the calmness in its voice and imagine, perhaps, an oak-panelled room with soft velvet curtains of faded rose pink at the windows, warm from the sun. Or baskets of dried flowers on an old stone hearth and oil paintings in gilded frames—glossy fruit piled high, ruddy apples, and golden pears—or cheerful, chubby children in an idyllic country scene. It is a comforting sound; even the whirring of its mechanism as it gathers itself to strike the hour is like the purring of a large, contented cat.

But then the girls heard someone coming up the stairs. The footsteps were accompanied by a cheerful tune: *'pom pom di pom-pom, pom po-pom po-pom... '* sang the voice as it came gradually nearer.

"I know that tune," said Holly. "It's the Toreador's Song from 'Carmen.' Don't you remember, Granny sang in it in the Easter holidays?

You know, that concert at the Dome Theatre. And I'm sure I know that voice."

It seemed that the owner of the voice would pass by the gallery, but then the footsteps stopped and turned back. In a moment, Mr. Edwards was standing beside them.

"Quite right, young lady," he said to Holly. "What a delight it is to know when one's 'pom di pom' is recognised. And did your granny enjoy singing in 'Carmen'?"

"Mr. Edwards!" Holly could have hugged him. "We thought you'd gone on holiday. We're so glad to see you!"

"We came specially to find you," added Beth, "because we didn't know what to do. And we've got loads to tell you. Miss Jones said you'd gone to Anda something."

"Andalucia, in Spain. Yes, so we should have done. My wife and I arrived at Gatwick only to be told that our flight, along with all the others this afternoon, was indefinitely delayed due to industrial action by the baggage handlers. I prefer to call it industrial inaction."

"That's *so* good! I mean, we're really sorry about your holiday and everything." Beth, feeling very embarrassed, turned to Holly for help.

"What Beth means is," said Holly, "you're the only person who can help us, and we were just really sad when we thought you'd gone away and…oh dear, I think I'm making it worse."

Mr. Edwards laughed. "Don't you worry. It's good to know when one is needed. So, while my wife awaits further news at home, and our bags remain packed and ready for a speedy return to Gatwick, what can I do to help? After such a greeting, I sincerely hope I will be able to help. Now, let's go over there and make ourselves comfortable."

He led the way to a semicircle of folding chairs grouped around a small table near the window. A number of leaflets lay on the table advertising attractions in the town. Beth nervously shuffled through some with a splendid photo of the Royal Pavilion on the front in an impossibly blue sky. She was still feeling embarrassed about her expressions of joy at seeing Mr. Edwards.

Neither of the girls knew how to begin. There was so much to tell; less than a day had passed since they'd left the world of 1915, but now it seemed like a lifetime away. Outside the open window, the patter of raindrops dripping mournfully from the tall lime tree mingled with the sound of traffic on wet roads.

"Can I take it, young ladies," asked Mr. Edwards, "that you have been on your travels again? Now, I don't want to rush you, but I

could, unlikely though it would seem, get a call requesting our immediate return to the airport, and I should hate to have to leave with an
untold story so much wanting to be told."

"Yes. Yes, we have." Holly was seized with panic at the thought
that their extraordinary luck in Mr. Edwards's unexpected presence
could be lost at any moment. "We've got *so* much to tell you. We've
had a brilliant adventure, and we've found out all sorts of things, and
we know who Josh is, and Amelia, and we met a German spy and—"

"Yes, and we know about the bells! You see, what happened was…
Amelia told us that… it was so funny and… but we still don't know
who Marjorie is and we really need to find out because she asked us
to go to… to Wales and… and… Holly doesn't know how to get the
photo back and…" Beth was speaking so fast that her words were
tumbling over each other.

"Whoa! Let's take it slowly. I don't want to miss anything, do I?
Just start at the beginning, if you can, and tell me all about it."

Mr. Edwards sat quietly without a single interruption other than a
nod of the head or an occasional "how splendid," or "my goodness
me," as they began to unfold the full story of their adventures. His
delight at hearing the story of the bells sparked a special request to
the girls.

"Write it down for me, will you? It's most important we don't lose
the story now that we have it at last. You see, later on you may think
of all this as a dream, or even as your vivid imagination playing
tricks. I know I did. I almost began to doubt whether my journey back
to 1876 had really happened, but then I was granted only one journey
back in time. How I would have loved to have gone back again, like
you did!"

"We did write it down," said Beth, "last night, when we went to
bed. We were scared we might forget."

"We were worried we might start to think it had never really happened. You never told us how you got back from 1876; will you tell
us?" asked Holly.

"Yes, I certainly will. But it can wait, even until I'm home from
Spain if necessary. You must finish telling me your story now."

The grey, damp day in 2001 seemed to disappear as they related
their adventure on the pier, the strange meeting with Gypsy Marigold,
and the capture of the German spy. Outside, the drizzle had turned
into diagonal streaks of needle sharp rain that splattered noisily on the
corrugated iron roof of the builder's hut below, but Holly and Beth
were oblivious to it and to the chilly wind blowing through the open

window as they were lost in the world of 1915. At last, they came to the questions they so urgently needed to ask Mr. Edwards.

"Can I help you find out who Marjorie is? Well, I will certainly do my best. We do have some good clues through her friends and what she told you about herself," said Mr. Edwards. "But the letter—now that's a tricky one. A letter that was posted eighty-six years ago would be very difficult indeed to trace. If it *was* posted to you—and you can't be certain about that, can you?—in all likelihood it would have been returned to the sender when you were not found at your address. However, there is a possibility…"

He never finished his sentence because at that moment he was interrupted by a shout from the other side of the gallery.

"Hi, Beth! Hi, Holly! What're you doing here? I thought you were going to France." It was Alice, hastily followed by her mother. "Oh hello, Mr. Edwards. Mum was looking for you. She wants to ask you something." Alice wore a bright orange cagoule over her flared jeans; little rivulets of water ran down off it onto the polished floor.

"I hope we're not interrupting anything," said Mrs. Bowman as she attempted to roll up her wet umbrella, causing almost as much damage as Alice's dripping cagoule. "I just wondered if you could tell me a bit about the little donkey cart on the ground floor. I believe it's something special." She smiled at Holly and Beth. "And how are you two, and Mum and Dad? Mum must be very busy getting ready for your holiday."

Go away, thought Holly, *please, please, go away.* But she answered as politely as possible. "We're fine. Mum's packing. We've just been doing some shopping." What could she do to make them go away? Beth glared and said nothing.

Mr. Edwards had stood up when Mrs. Bowman and Alice arrived.

"The donkey cart is indeed something special," he said, "and I should be delighted to tell you about it."

No, thought Beth, *no, no, no! How could you do this to us?*

Just as she thought she was about to burst with frustration, Mr. Edwards added, "But first I must answer some of the questions that Holly and Beth have asked me. They are interested in learning about old Brighton, and they have asked for my help. I will be with you as soon as I can."

"I'll wait here, Mum, if you're going downstairs again," said Alice. She settled herself down on the chair next to Beth and began picking up the Royal Pavilion brochures and arranging them in neat patterns.

Beth was screaming inside. In her mind's eye, she could see Miss Jones running up the stairs calling out to Mr. Edwards with a message from the airport, or maybe his mobile phone would ring and he'd just say he'd have to go, and that would be that. No mystery solved, no chance of tracing the letter and the photo or finding out anything more about Marjorie. Stupidly, she felt tears coming into her eyes. She'd made a friend, a good friend who liked to dance like she did, and she'd lost her, and she'd never see her again. What would Marjorie have thought when they never came back, never answered any letters, never went to visit her and Peter in Wales?

Beth rushed to the window and let the rain and the cold wind blow in her face. She felt unbearably sad. Part of her wanted to tell Alice all about it; she'd tried once before, right at the beginning of their adventures, but she'd pretended it was a story that she'd made up because she'd wanted to keep Marjorie all to herself. And now Alice would never believe her.

But then, to her utter joy, she heard Mr. Edwards saying: "Meanwhile, might I suggest that you take Alice to see the new exhibit in the Bronze Age gallery? It's a collection of remarkable jewellery, beautifully preserved. We're very proud of it."

Reluctantly, Alice followed her enthusiastic mother out of the gallery. She stared back at Beth; there was some mystery going on, she was sure of it.

"So, where were we?" continued Mr. Edwards. "Ah yes, the letter. Now, it is just possible—and I must tell you, so that you will not be disappointed, that this is the very smallest of chances—that the owners of your house in 1915 might have thought that the name Randall on the letter could refer to the family who owned the Dahlia nursery—your family. Now if this were so—and it is a very big if—they might have forwarded it to Randall's Nurseries."

"Daddy's got an old tin box with lots of old letters and things in it," Holly said, hardly daring to hope, "and birth certificates and stuff, and old photos of the nursery from his grandfather's time. Do you think it really could be in there?"

"Well, now, you mustn't raise your hopes too much because, after all, it is much more likely that the letter and the photo were thrown away long, long ago when they were not recognised as belonging to your family. But you could certainly look. Now, the other possibility is also very much an outside chance. Did you not tell me, Holly, that there was a lady in the photograph with you?"

"Yes, and I know who she is! There's a photo of her downstairs—she was a nurse at the Indian hospital in the Pavilion, and she was called Florence Anselm. It says so in the newspaper."

"Anselm," repeated Mr. Edwards thoughtfully. "There was an Anselm family who owned a chemist's shop in King's Road until quite recently. It's not a very common name. I might be able to find out if any member of the family still lives in Brighton. You see, it's just possible that if Florence Anselm saw the photo displayed at the photographer's on the prom, she might have bought a copy herself. Leave it to me; as soon as I return from my holiday, I shall make enquiries."

"Oh, but…" began Beth.

"I'm sorry, I can do nothing before then. As you know, I should be in Spain now." Mr. Edwards had guessed what Beth was about to say. "But I promise I will find out whatever I can just as soon as possible. Now, is there anything else you would like to ask me?"

"Yes. I was just thinking," said Holly, "you once said that, when we were in Marjorie's time, we were 'there by grace.' What did you mean? I'm still not really sure, although once or twice I thought I knew."

"Well now, I imagine it's nothing you've done or had to do that gave you that door into the past," answered Mr. Edwards. "I believe it was a gift, a very loving gift, and that's what I meant by grace. And you accepted it. On that first day when Marjorie called at your beach hut, you could have insisted that she'd come to the wrong one, and then she would have gone away and probably you would never have seen her again. But you didn't. You made her welcome, you offered her your Jaffa Cakes, and you stepped into her world as friends, even though you were a bit scared."

Holly was asking more questions, but now the conversation was getting rather serious and Beth's attention began to wander. She found herself thinking about the doll in the pram just across the room from them; she'd been so sure it was Jack, but now horrid little niggling doubts were creeping in uninvited. Maybe the drumming of the rain outside and the greyness of the afternoon were affecting her mood. *After all,* she thought, *why should he really be Jack?* Perhaps Holly was right; there were probably hundreds of dolls made just like him. And anyway, Marjorie lived in London and then she went to Wales, so what would he be doing in Brighton? Maybe she'd imagined the whole thing, and Marjorie had never told her anything about her doll. Maybe she'd imagined everything! Perhaps Holly was talking about a story she'd read, and they hadn't ever really met Marjorie and her friends at all.

Beth was about to get up and walk away. She'd go downstairs and try to find Alice; at least she knew Alice was real.

Then suddenly, as often happens in an English summer, the rain ceased and in the space of a few seconds the grey clouds parted and a shaft of bright sunlight streamed through the window. A thrush, perched high on a branch of the tall lime tree, began its happy song, and a sparkling prism from the chandelier, which hung on a long chain from the ceiling of the gallery, reflected every colour of the rainbow as the sunlight touched it. No magic in all the world could have caused such a transformation. Beth's dark mood immediately began to lift.

And what was Mr. Edwards saying now? He was back in 1876, and the train bearing Queen Victoria herself was approaching the station. Beth had to listen.

There he was, an eighteen-year-old boy again, standing on the platform at Upper Winterbourne amidst the excited, expectant crowd. A shrill whistle signalled that the Royal Train was almost there. A hush fell over the crowd as if it held its breath in anticipation. Above the tops of the golden beech trees, puffs of smoke from the approaching engine dissolved into the crisp, bright air.

Mrs. Jameson, holding tightly to her husband's arm lest in her excitement she should slip right over the platform edge onto the rails, released her grip for a moment to open the carpetbag at her feet. She drew out a small union jack on a stick and thrust it into young Mr. Edwards's hands. He waved it high above his head and for a moment he could see nothing in front of him but a sea of red, white and blue. It seemed that every man, woman and child had at least one flag to wave; some had two.

As the beautiful, glossy black engine with its shiny brass funnel and trappings pulled into the station, a great cheer arose from the crowd: "God Save Her Majesty! Long Live the Queen!"

Queen Victoria stepped from the train in the most dignified manner, helped by her courtiers, alighting just inches from where the Jamesons and Mr. Edwards were standing. A tiny figure, she was dressed in a black satin gown with a fur-edged cape over her shoulders and a small fur cap on top of her white hair. It was held in place by a jet hatpin, which caught the light just as Mrs. Jameson's earrings had done.

The Queen's face was solemn, even a little severe. But then, just as the dignitaries of the railway company stepped up to greet her, to the Jamesons' horror, their Yorkshire terrier bounded forward, leapt a full twelve inches in the air, and gave a little yap of greeting to the Queen.

Immediately, her solemn expression relaxed into a beaming smile, which so transformed her that the dignitaries, who were all ready to scold the dog and the Jamesons alike, began to laugh.

Mr. Edwards was startled to become aware that Queen Victoria was looking directly at him, and hers were twinkling eyes, so unlike the serious portraits of her in her later years. He could almost have sworn she winked at him!

Now, what happened next happened very suddenly. Whether it was the extraordinary brightness of the sun in his eyes, the chill of the air, or just the excitement of the moment, he wasn't sure, but he began to sneeze. He couldn't stop sneezing, and when the sneeze turned into a tickly cough, Mr. Jameson whispered to him that perhaps he should fetch a drink of water from the station buffet. Struggling to control his cough, he weaved his way through the crowd to reach the frosted glass doors, through which he had come earlier that morning, and pushed them open.

"And that, sadly and abruptly, ended my adventure," said Mr. Edwards. "The buffet was just as I'd left it: the rock cakes and the Petit Beurre biscuits on their glass shelf, my empty Tizer bottle still on the table, and the tea lady behind the counter as cheerful as ever.

"I remember she saw my expression of horror and called out 'forgotten something, laddie? Is anything the matter?' I just shook my head, pushed the doors open again, and rushed onto the platform. There were my school friends and all our luggage. I couldn't understand it; nobody seemed to have noticed my absence, and surely the train should have come by now? Then I looked at the clock, which seemed to have diminished in size and now stood at two minutes to nine o'clock, only three minutes since I'd arrived in 1876. My adventure was over, but in a way it was only just beginning." He paused and closed his eyes for a moment as if to see the scene better in his mind.

But Holly and Beth would hear no more because at that moment Miss Jones, looking somewhat flustered, came hurrying across the gallery towards them.

"Mr. Edwards, it's your wife on the phone. Your flight has been rescheduled for six o'clock this evening. She says would you please hurry home as soon as possible. I'm so sorry to trouble you, but she seemed a little anxious." She acknowledged Holly and Beth with a

fleeting smile; her earlier insistence that Mr. Edwards was not at the
museum caused her some embarrassment.

"Quite right too," said Mr. Edwards. "Would you tell her, please,
that I'm on way?"

Miss Jones, almost at a run but more at a trot, left to attend to the
telephone.

"Well, young ladies, we were just in time. And I must be in good
time to resume my holiday. But on my return, and yours, we will for-
mulate a plan of action, and who knows what wonders we may discover? Now I must say goodbye. Enjoy your holiday in France; I'm
sure it will be a most exciting time for you all."

He'd been gone only a few moments when Beth remembered
something, for her doubts and disbelief had vanished in that shaft of
sunlight.

She ran after him, through the gallery and down the stairs, just in
time to catch him in the hallway. His hand was already on the swing
door when she called out to him, slightly out of breath, "Mr.
Edwards! I forgot to ask you about the doll, the new one in the doll's
pram upstairs." Visitors arriving at the museum frowned in disap-
proval at the noise, so Beth quickly lowered her voice as she reached
the door. "He's a boy doll. Can you tell us where he came from?"

"He's a fine little fellow, isn't he? Indeed I can. He arrived only last
week. An elderly lady by the name of Miss Prudence Shotley brought
him in. She is the youngest of three sisters; the other two have, alas,
died. She was moving into sheltered accommodation and had to dis-
pose of a number of her possessions."

"But was he her doll? I mean, had she always had him?" Beth desperately needed more information. Now she was so sure he'd been
Marjorie's.

"As a matter of fact, no. She told me that when she was about six
years old, a friend of her eldest sister had given him to her to look
after—'to keep him safe always' she'd been told. She'd taken great
care of him all her life but, sadly, she'd never married and had no one
left to entrust him to, so she brought him to us. His name, she said,
is—"

"Jack. It's Jack," said Beth, now joined by Holly in the hall.

If Mr. Edwards was surprised by this, he didn't show it. He smiled
and nodded, then quickly turned and hurried out of the door and down
the steps onto the path.

18

"Have you seen my MaxMara T-shirt? I can't find it anywhere!"

Holly had been delving into her cupboards and drawers, and now a small pile of random shorts, T-shirts, skirts and jeans littered the floor by her bed.

"Your what?" called out Beth from the next room amidst the noise of drawers slamming and the clatter of coat hangers.

"The one Granny bought me in Milan. You know, the white one with the gold on the front."

Holly was getting annoyed. She'd already spent half the morning trying to find her camera that had somehow found its way into her sock drawer.

"Oh, that one. Er, I thought you'd given it to me. You said—"

"Beth, hand it over!"

Holly stormed into her sister's room, snatched the T-shirt that Beth was guiltily holding, went back to her bedroom, slammed the door, and turned on Radio 1 full blast.

"Girls! Turn it down!" Katy yelled from the kitchen. "I can't hear myself think. I'm trying to make a list here of things I haven't done yet which are *desperately urgent.*"

She stressed the last two words in an attempt to make an impression on her less than cooperative daughters. *Really,* she thought, *is it all worth it?* The pre-holiday stress was beginning to get to her, and the girls had been in a funny mood since they'd returned from the town the day before. There was a definite lack of enthusiasm, which was odd considering that this was to be their first trip abroad. *Oh well,* she thought as she finished her list and started to gather together necessities for the journey the next day, *it's probably just the weather.* Now, if it had stayed bright and sunny like yesterday evening had turned out to be, they'd surely be feeling in quite a different mood and be bouncing through the packing with happy smiles. Well, something like that.

She glanced through the kitchen window at the lowering grey sky. Maybe there was a storm brewing. It would certainly explain the nagging headache she felt beginning at the back of her left eye. Almost immediately, a faint rumble confirmed her fears. Katy sighed and went to fetch a glass of water. Perhaps a long drink would help; it sometimes did. She envied Stephen. He would just come home at the end of the day, albeit very late—he'd taken his bicycle this morning; she did hope he'd remembered the lamps—to find everything packed and ready, the car filled with petrol, oil and water checked, and all he'd have to do the next morning would be to get into the car with them all and drive off.

A single flash of lightning made Katy jump. And then the phone rang.

Upstairs, Holly and Beth had almost finished their packing. Beth was just struggling to do up the zip on her holdall—with Holly's help, in spite of her anger at the stolen T-shirt and protestations that Beth couldn't possibly need six hard-back books for a week's holiday—when they heard their mother talking on the phone.

"So how is she now? Oh dear, I'm so sorry... no, of course we will... don't worry, we'll get it all done somehow... no, I know you don't."

There was a pause. "What's Mummy talking about?" whispered Beth. "Do you think Aunty Rachel's okay? I hope the baby's okay."

Holly nodded. She looked worried.

Katy was talking again. "Honestly, it's okay. We don't have to leave until about ten tomorrow morning... yes, we'll phone tonight and let you know. Give lots of love to Rachel, won't you? Yes, and to Dad. Bye for now."

Beth was first down the stairs.

"What's happened, Mummy? Is Aunty Rachel okay? Has she had the baby?"

"We heard you talking. We were worried something had happened," Holly added.

"It's not Aunty Rachel, she's fine," said Katy, sitting down at the kitchen table. The girls joined her. "She's going into hospital tomorrow for the baby to be induced. That means the doctor will give her something to help her go into labour. It's just because she's eleven days overdue, that's all. She's doing fine." Katy paused. She took a deep breath. "No, it's Great-Granny."

"She's not—" Holly felt an awful sinking feeling in her stomach. Part of her wanted to run away; she didn't want to hear what her mother was going to say. She thought again of the quiet bungalow in Rottingdean and the empty sofa bed. Beth looked shaken.

"No, no." Katy laughed, a little falsely and uneasily, and shook her head. "But she is very poorly. Granny's really worried about her because she's had a phone call from the nursing home to say that Great-Granny's not eating and seems very depressed. She's not been able to speak since the stroke, so it's difficult for the staff to know what the problem is. It must be so awful not to be able to communicate with people."

Katy rubbed her forehead. The headache was getting worse, and she was afraid the girls wouldn't like what she was going to say next.

"So, I said we'd go and visit her. Matron thinks that seeing people she knows will help."

"What, now? Today?" Beth was horrified. "But she lives hundreds of miles away! What about all the packing? You said you'd got loads to do"

Beth didn't enjoy long car journeys and frequently felt sick. The Elders Nursing Home where Great-Granny lived was in Dorset. Last time they went, they had to stop twice—once for Beth to be sick, and the other time for her to walk around until the fresh air made her feel better.

"I know, darling, and so I have," said Katy. "But how could we go off to France not knowing how Great-Granny is and thinking that maybe we could have helped her feel better? We've got to go, even if we're packing all night."

Holly said, "Do you think you ought to go without us? What if she's so poorly that, well..."

"Definitely not. I think you two could be a great help. She sees old people all the time. I think very few children visit where she is now. It is important, it really is," said Katy, "and sometimes, when you do something that's really going to help someone and you give them your time, somehow you get it back again. It's a funny thing, but it happens. Maybe it's God's way of saying thank you."

"You mean we get it by grace?" asked Beth.

Her mother was surprised. It was a strange thing for Beth to say; she wondered where she'd heard the expression. "Well, yes, that's right," she said. "So, are you on for it? Should Operation Florence Nightingale commence?"

All at once their spirits lifted, in spite of the thought of finishing the packing in the middle of the night. Even the grey sky seemed a little less sombre and there'd not been another clap of thunder since that first distant rumble. Katy felt her headache beginning to ease.

Holly and Beth looked at each other. There wasn't really a choice, was there?

"In that case, course we're on," said Holly. "What d'you want us to do? Shall we go and lock up now? Or I could make some sandwiches for us to take with us, and some tea."

"There's no fresh bread left in the house because I've been trying to use it all up before we went away. Don't worry, we'll stop at a motorway service station for lunch, but I'll make a thermos of tea to take with us in case we need to stop again later. It's all minor roads once you turn off the motorway and there's nowhere to get anything. I'll put some biscuits in, too."

"Okay, we'll lock up. Come on, Holly, we've got to hurry up." Beth pushed the thoughts of carsickness from her mind and threw herself into organising mode. The sooner they left, the sooner the long journey would be over and they'd be back home again.

"That'd be good. We certainly need to leave as soon as possible." Katy went to put the kettle on. "I'll phone Daddy to tell him what's happened and then the nursing home to let them know we're coming."

Upstairs, the girls busied themselves with tidying their beds and noisily shutting all the windows.

"If only Great-Granny could talk," sighed Holly, as she pulled the cat out from under her bed to take downstairs. "Even if she's not old enough to have been alive in 1915, she might have been able to help us."

"Let's tell her about it all anyway," said Beth. "I don't think Mummy'll try to stop us because it's good for people like that to be talked to, isn't it? I saw something on 'Blue Peter' about it. It was about people in commas or something."

Holly laughed. "Comas, stupid," she said, borrowing Beth's expression. "Not commas!"

§§§§§

The traffic out of Brighton was heavy and slow. Travelling west on the A27 seemed to be nothing but a succession of roundabouts and traffic lights with only a few clear stretches in between where Katy could pick up some speed. By the time they reached the M27 it had eased considerably, but by then they were very hungry and stopped at the first Little Chef restaurant they could find. But when Katy was told there would be a twenty-minute wait for service, she walked out. They were all wondering whether they could keep going for much longer; Beth had already started on the biscuits and was threatening to pour herself a cup of tea while the car was travelling at 70 mph. Luckily, they didn't have far to go before the next Little Chef, and, to their relief, it was half empty and they were ushered to a table straightaway.

Forty minutes later, feeling refreshed after cheese omelettes with chips and salad, they were on their way again. As they travelled west, the threat of a storm drifted farther and farther away and, for a brief moment, a small patch of blue appeared between the clouds. It didn't last, but the rain had stopped, and the dry roads ahead of them indicated that this part of the south had managed to miss it altogether.

The Elders Nursing Home was just outside a small market town called Lower Gladon. It was usually quite a sleepy place, except for a week in July when an annual pop festival drew crowds to Blacksmith's Farm on the southern side of town. But today, with just over a mile to go, the traffic was building up. When it slowed to 10 mph, Katy was beginning to get impatient.

"It must be road works," she said, "or an accident or something. This is going to take hours, and we haven't got hours." For the first time that afternoon, she began to question the wisdom of her last minute decision to drive all this way when they were leaving for France the next morning. Maybe her heart had ruled her head just a bit too much. The girls were being very quiet, but Beth let out a deep sigh.

"Holly, can you look at the map and see if you can find us a diversion? I'm getting really worried about the time—I can't think what's going on here." She drummed her fingers on the steering wheel and opened the window further for some more air. It was becoming very warm, but the air smelled polluted from the now almost stationary traffic.

The girls pored over the map. Holly said, "I think if you take the next turning left, just past a bridge, we should be able to get to a B road which goes straight into town. I think." Map reading wasn't her strongest point. "Actually," she added, "it's not even a B road, it's one of those thin black lines on the map."

"Well, anything's going to be better than this. We might as well try it."

A quarter of a mile and twenty minutes farther on, Katy turned the car off the main road on to a single-track lane with high hedges on either side. At first, the diversion seemed a good one, until the tower of Lower Gladon Church came in sight and they joined another queue of stop-go traffic. But now the reason for it became clear: a big banner, suspended between two barns on the right, advertised 'Lower Gladon Farmers' Market and Steam Fair. 3pm - 8pm TODAY.'

Soon they could see ahead as the road dropped steeply towards the town. There were tractors, steam rollers, and trucks piled high with produce at the front of the long row of Land Rovers and cars which stretched for about half a mile down the hill.

In desperation, Katy took the next lane to the left, which was not much wider than a farm track, and to their utter astonishment they found themselves, just ten minutes later, joining another lane running directly into town.

But as they reached the Market Place, the road was blocked with a diversion sign. By now, the sun had broken through, and the temperature had risen sharply.

"I can't bear it! I'm going to try anything now," said Katy, pushing her sweat-damp hair off her forehead.

There was a drive on the left that ran into the backyard of an off-licence. She swung sharply into it, with just inches to spare on either side between the car and a wall on the left and a wicket fence on the right.

"Mummy! What're you *doing?*" Beth, who had started to feel sick before they hit the local traffic, was beginning to turn very pale.

"If we can just get through here," Katy was driving down what seemed to be a private driveway, "I can actually see The Elders just beyond that hedge over there. This won't be on the map."

Holly was clutching the back of the front passenger seat and didn't dare look. She shut her eyes and waited for the horrible scraping sound that was sure to come as Katy edged the car agonisingly close to the wall. All thoughts of the adventures she'd been so longing to relate to her great-grandmother were pushed from her mind.

But, incredibly, they emerged without a scratch. "There, I told you so!" Katy laughed out loud. "We've made it. Look, here's the drive to the nursing home. We'll be there in two minutes."

§ § § § §

They parked on the gravel drive next to The Elders' blue minibus. Beth stepped from the car looking dazed, but the colour was returning to her cheeks. Holly, on Katy's instruction, pushed the brass button on the wall next to the glass-panelled front door. They could hear the bell echoing down the hallway, but no one came.

The house was about two hundred years old and built of a warm golden stone; it had once been the Manor House of Lower Gladon. A magnificent Magnolia Grandiflora grew against the front wall, reaching up to a row of elegant white-painted sash windows. Through one wide-open window they could hear a television or radio playing. They waited, but still no one came.

"Ring again," said Katy.

This time, Beth pressed the brass bell push. At last it was answered by the sound of approaching footsteps hurrying along the hall. A young nurse in a starched white uniform and with an unsmiling face pulled back several bolts, finally opening the door no more than a crack.

"Yes? Can I help you?" She didn't sound as if she wanted to.

"I'm Katy Randall, and these are my daughters. We've come to see my grandmother, Mrs. Granger."

"You are very late." She spoke with a strong accent and wore a badge with the name 'Reetta Koseff' on her lapel. "We expect you one hour before. Mrs. Granger, she is asleep. She sleeps always between three and five. I cannot disturb her; it is not good for her. Please, you come back."

"No, we can't. This is ridiculous," said Katy. "We've driven hours to get here in ghastly traffic. I demand to see her NOW!"

Holly and Beth had never heard their mother speak like that before. They didn't know whether to laugh or cry, so they stayed rooted to the spot and kept quiet.

"Please, you wait." The girl disappeared, shutting the door firmly behind her.

"I don't believe this. I just don't believe it!" Katy was furious.

"Do you think they'll let us in?" asked Holly.

"Oh yes, they'll let us in all right if I have anything to do with it. But they'd better hurry up or I'll...I'll...well, I'll just have to find another way in."

Somewhere above them a sash window opened, and for a second or two a strain of 1950s dance band music drifted down to them, and then the sash was closed again. Katy stepped back and looked up at the window, shielding her eyes against the sun. She seemed to be looking along the row of windows and then at the Grandiflora, which was in full bloom, its enormous creamy white flowers and dark glossy foliage almost touching the panes of two of the windows.

"Mummy! You're never going to try and climb up the magnolia!" Holly was horrified. "You can't. You'll…"

"I can," said Beth, "I'm really good at ropes in the gym. I'll climb up, and I'll climb into that open window, then I'll come down, and I'll open the door for you. We'll find Great-Granny and… and…

"No, I don't think so!" laughed Katy. "You'd give some poor old lady a heart attack. Pity we don't know which window is the landing one, though."

"Mummy!" said Holly. "You don't mean it!"

As it happened, she never found out because at that moment the door was opened by a large woman wearing a white uniform similar to Reetta's, but with a wide blue belt round her waist, fastened with a silver buckle. She wore a little white cap on her grey curly hair and a watch pinned to her chest, which Beth noticed was upside down.

"Mrs. Randall. I'm Matron Sonia Watson. I spoke on the phone to your mother in Canada this morning." She held out her hand to Katy and the girls. "Do please come in. I do apologise for Reetta's rudeness. She's new to us, and she didn't understand."

The repentant but rather sulky Reetta stood at Matron's side. A ridiculous notion came into Holly's mind that she was about to curtsey to them; she found herself trying to suppress a giggle.

They followed Matron down the oak-floored hallway, passing several doors with numbers on them, some standing ajar. There was a smell of polish and lavender and, from somewhere in the distance, fried bacon.

"You know, don't you," she said quietly as they walked along, "that your grandmother hasn't been able to speak since her stroke?" Katy nodded. "We are very concerned, too, about her lack of appetite, but I'm sure your visit will do her the world of good." She stopped outside the last door but one. "Here we are," she said. "Just knock and go on in. Reetta will bring some tea for you."

The door was marked 11 in brass numbers and stood half open with a wedge under it to stop it from closing. There was no sound from within. They could see the back of a moss-green winged armchair and, on the right, a mahogany tallboy. Under the window was a small bookcase, on top of which were several silver-framed photos. The long pale yellow curtains moved slightly in the breeze.

Katy knocked gently; to knock louder seemed intrusive. There was no reply, so they quietly entered the room. Beth was clutching a bunch of flowers Katy had hastily picked from the garden that morning. She'd wrapped the stalks carefully in wet paper towels and polythene and, remarkably, they had survived the journey.

Mrs. Granger was sitting in the armchair, apparently asleep. In spite of the warmth of the afternoon, she had a crocheted rug over her knees; her head was to one side, resting on the wing of the chair. Her white hair was in soft waves, and her cheeks were quite pink, despite her lack of appetite.

Katy pulled up a wicker chair which stood by the window and sat down very close to her grandmother. She took her hand, leaned forward and kissed her cheek. Holly and Beth sat on the bed, feeling subdued and sad. The old lady looked so frail.

"Granny, it's me," said Katy gently, "and Holly and Beth. We've come to see you.

19

Mrs. Granger stirred a little. Although her eyelids remained closed, Katy felt a distinct squeeze on her hand.

"She knows we're here," said Katy to the girls. "Talk to her. I'm sure she'd like to hear your voices."

"Shall we?" whispered Holly to Beth. Beth nodded. "Okay. Great-Granny, we've got lots to tell you. It's all about something that happened to us when we were in the beach hut. One day, about three weeks ago, a little girl came and knocked on the door and she came in and…"

"Had tea with us," said Beth. "Well, it wasn't exactly tea because Mum had gone to get it, but she had some Jaffa Cakes with us and then when we went out again it was 1914. Only we didn't know it was."

"Yes, and the First World War was about to start," added Holly. "You might have been just alive then, Great-Granny."

Katy laughed, a little uneasily. "They've been dreaming," she said, "or daydreaming. But they're determined to tell you about their make-believe world, and they're very good at it. They nearly had me taken in." Katy felt another squeeze, and Mrs. Granger's left hand moved slightly to clutch at the pastel-coloured crocheted rug.

And so Holly and Beth told their story, right down to the smallest detail. Between them, with constant interruptions and corrections from each other, it took some time to tell. A rather subdued Reetta brought tea and biscuits, and later the sun began to sink very gradually in the west and the shadows cast by the golden rays streaming

161

through the sash windows began to lengthen. Several times Mrs. Granger moved; once her eyelids fluttered and another time she opened her mouth a little as if she were about to speak, but no sound came. Katy was afraid the girls were tiring her. She asked her grandmother if she would like to rest, but she shook her head and moved the fingers of one hand in such a way as to indicate that she'd like them to continue. Katy tried to hold a cup of tea for her to drink, but she firmly refused it.

At last, they came to the very end of the story.

"And Mr. Edwards is going to help us again when he gets back," said Beth. "He says he's got more clues now to help us find out who Marjorie is."

In the telling of their adventures to their great-grandmother, the girls had not once tried to disguise the name of their friend as they had to their mother on that very first day. Katy listened in amazement. She'd overheard them discussing their so-called adventures, but never with such clarity or such detail. She felt utterly lost for words.

In the brief silence that followed the end of the story, Mrs. Granger gave a little cough, pulled herself up in her chair, and opened her eyes. She blinked at the strong sunlight and coughed again as if she were trying to clear her voice to speak. Katy, her heart pounding, leaned very close to her.

"No," Mrs. Granger struggled for the words to come. "No... dream...."

Her voice was no more than a whisper. She sank back in her chair again, exhausted from the effort, but with a tremulous smile on her lips.

"Oh, Granny, you spoke!" Katy, still holding her hand, leaned forward and hugged her grandmother. "You did, we heard you, didn't we, girls?"

Holly took her other hand and Beth, not knowing quite what to do, stroked her soft white hair as if she would their cat. Mrs. Granger smiled again and gave Holly's hand a squeeze.

Then hesitantly and with great effort, she said, "Wait... com... ing... rest a moment."

Time seemed to stand still as they waited for the old lady to summon all her strength to speak. They could hear the murmur of bees in the magnolia outside the window and below them the puttering of an electric mower. Somewhere in the distance, the faint sounds of music and voices from the Steam Fair were carried on the breeze.

Now Mrs. Granger was speaking again, this time more confidently. She looked lovingly at them all and addressed the girls.

"Do you..." she paused, pulling herself up a little again in her chair, "do you think... think... it was a dream?"

"No, it all happened, it really did, but only Mr. Edwards believed us," said Holly. "But now you believe us, don't you, Great-Granny?"

"Were you alive in 1914?" asked Beth excitedly. "Do you remember the war and stuff?"

Mrs. Granger nodded and patted Beth's hand.

It was like a miracle. Suddenly, unbelievably, their great-grandmother began to speak, at first quietly and slowly and with great care, but soon almost as they had known her before the stroke deprived her of speech. It was as if her voice had been unlocked after a long imprisonment.

"Holly, dear, you see my little bookshelf under the window? Look... look in the top shelf and take out for me the book on the left. It's the one that's..." She paused again, as if beginning to tire. Katy was worried; she could feel her grandmother's pulse quickening as she held her hand. "...that's taller than the others. It has a pale cover with... with patterns round... round the edge."

"Granny, are you all right?" asked Katy anxiously. "You mustn't tire yourself. Can I get you anything? I could call Matron?"

"No, darling, I'm all right. It's just that I'm not used to... to... my voice. It sounds strange to me. But I've been waiting a long time. Such a long time."

"I'm really sorry. The traffic was awful," said Katy. "It took us ages longer than it should have done. There was a Farmers' Market and a Steam Fair and..."

Mrs. Granger shook her head. "Why fret about them if today be sweet?" she said, as she put her hand on Katy's arm to stop her. Katy was puzzled; she didn't understand what she was talking about. She wondered if her grandmother's mind was becoming confused. "No, no, it's all right, darling. That was, well, it was really no wait at all. Yes, that's the one," she said to Holly, who had taken the book from the bookshelf.

Holly didn't move. She stood there by the window, holding the book in both hands, staring down at it. It was the Rubaiyat of Omar Khayam.

"Come on, stupid," said Beth, getting up and going to grab the book. "Great-Granny wants the book—why don't you bring it over?

Oh, Great-Granny! It's the book Amelia had for her birthday, the one
we told you about."

"Yes, darling. And that Christmas, Mother and Daddy gave me this
one." Mrs. Granger spoke so softly that they had to listen very carefully. "They thought it was a bit grown-up for me, but I wanted it so
much. Such strange words and beautiful pictures. I was so thrilled.
I've always treasured that book."

And then Holly felt prickles all over her and a little shiver down
her spine. It wasn't an unpleasant sensation; it just seemed to paralyse
her as if she were in a dream. She looked at her great-grandmother
and just for a second–or more a fraction of a split second, like a fleeting thought that flashes across the memory–she saw, not a white-
haired old lady crippled by a stroke, but a little girl in a navy serge
dress with a white sailor collar, a blue ribbon tied in her brown hair; a
little girl with laughing eyes, swinging her feet as if she were dancing.

"Marjorie?" whispered Holly, "Marjorie?" And then the moment
was gone.

Beth stared at Holly, took the book from her rigid hands and put it
in Mrs. Granger's lap. Her mind was in a whirl; thoughts kept tumbling over each other, over and over and becoming more and more
tangled up. She needed to think clearly, but she couldn't. What had
Holly just said? No, no! How could her own great-grandmother be
Marjorie? That's just silly; that's impossible. And yet here was the
book, the same as the one she'd seen Amelia unwrap on the beach
only two days ago. She watched in silence as the old lady picked it
up.

"Thank you, dear," said Mrs. Granger. "Now, Holly, there's something special here for you. Can you come and see?"

Holly tried to move; she forced one foot an inch or two, then the
other, and at last her feet obeyed her and she was able to walk across
the room. She sat down on the bed. Her hands were shaking. She
turned them over and looked at them as if they were something
strange not belonging to her. Mrs. Granger carefully opened the pre-
cious book and took from its pages a battered brown envelope. She
handed it to Holly.

"Open it, darling," she said.

The old envelope bore a red one-penny stamp depicting the head of
King George V and was clearly postmarked 1pm 28 May 1915. It was
addressed in a careful copperplate hand to Mrs. Rowe, 53, Arthur
Road, London SW17, but had been re-addressed twice and had two

earlier, barely legible postmarks underneath. Miss Holly Randall, 27, Nightingale Road, Brighton had been crossed out and Randall's Dahlia Nurseries put in its place. But the envelope had been marked 'Not known at this address. Return to sender'.

Inside was a faded sepia photograph of a young girl seated in a chair with a monkey on her shoulder, a fez perched ridiculously on its head. A young woman in a pretty straw hat was standing beside her, and in the distance was the West Pier, resplendent with flags flying.

"My photograph! Oh, Great-Granny, it *is* you. It is, isn't it?" Holly spoke in a voice that sounded to her as if it came from a long way off. "You *are* Marjorie—you really are Marjorie."

And now she found she could move properly; she flung her arms round her great-grandmother's neck, tears streaming down her face.

"But Marjorie's not an old lady!" Beth spoke almost angrily. "How can you be her? Marjorie's my friend, she's nine years old. We danced together!"

She rushed to the window and stared out. She needed to think but her head was still spinning, and the same thought kept coming back: it had been only the day before yesterday they'd played together on the beach. It couldn't happen, it just couldn't. She would put it out of her mind.

She leaned out, feeling the warm sun on her face. She watched as the big mower cut a path through a wild garden at the side of the lawn, a broad green stripe through the tall buttercups and clover amongst the waving grasses. Then the mower disappeared as it turned a corner round the side of the house. Beth wondered if the old people would ever walk on it. It looked exciting, as if it were leading somewhere; it made her want to go out and run along it, round the corner through to she didn't know where. She watched, half expecting the mower to reappear, but the sound died away as it continued its path into an unseen part of the garden.

Beth's head was becoming clearer now, and the idea came to her that that's what had happened in the beach hut when Marjorie came knocking on the door. They'd opened it and then somehow they'd stepped out onto an unknown path and round a corner—although of course it wasn't actually a corner—into an unseen world and an amazing adventure. Beth didn't understand any of it, it was all a mystery to her, but maybe it was meant to happen *because* Marjorie was really their great-granny, so that they would see that she wasn't just a very old lady who couldn't walk anymore and had to be pushed around in a wheelchair, but had once been just like them. How she must be longing to be able to dance again!

So Beth turned round and came back to her great-grandmother with tears in her eyes now.

"You must hate us. We never came back, and we said we would. We never wrote or anything. We couldn't because…because…I tried to tell you, didn't I? I tried to say we'd come from the future. We said we never would, but I just *had* to."

"And I laughed, didn't I, and said I'd come through the bandstand from 1066? You know, when you are very old, like me, you begin to remember things that happened a long, long time ago so very clearly. I can remember it so well! I've never forgotten you and now you have come back," said Great-Granny, with her arms round both the girls. "Don't you remember what I said to you on the prom? That I knew we'd meet again even if we were very old ladies?"

"Yes, but we never thought you'd be an old lady and we'd still be children," said Holly. "It sounds like a fairy story. Mummy, you must believe us now?"

Katy was speechless. Surely she must be dreaming? That was it; she was so tired after the long drive, and it was so warm she must have fallen asleep in her granny's bedroom. What a wonderful dream it was! Her own granny playing on the beach with Holly and Beth, a child again herself. What a lovely dream. How Granny would have loved that. Katy thought she must pinch herself to try to wake up; there wasn't time for a long sleep now. She tried, but nothing happened. She closed her eyes and opened them again, but everything looked just the same.

Mrs. Granger saw the confused look in her granddaughter's eyes. "Katy, dear," she said, "thank you for bringing my little friends back to me. And now I find they are my own. Together we can tell you much more so that you can be happy for us. Oh, how I wish your grandpa could have been here with us. How he would have loved to have known Holly and Beth and heard all about our adventures! But I don't know if he would have believed us. In those days…" She paused. The girls had never known their great-grandfather for he had died the year before Holly was born, but she smiled as she remembered him. "In those days," she continued, "when we were all younger, he used to say, didn't he, Katy, that we were always making up stories and laughing. Your mother would remember, I know she would." She settled back more comfortably in her armchair, pulling the rug further up her lap again.

Katy said, "Yes, oh yes, I remember too. Very well." She still felt as if she were dreaming as she tucked in the rug and plumped up the cushion behind the old lady's head, but then she found herself saying: "It's all true, isn't it? Everything the girls told me?"

"Yes, darling," Mrs. Granger answered quietly. "You will tell your mother, won't you? But of course you will. My little friends here will see to that." She closed her eyes for a moment, as if trying to see that far off world of her childhood again. "Oh, how I loved our beach hut! Well, it was Josh's parents' beach hut really, but we used to play pretend games in it, imagining it to be our own little house. Dulcie and I made up such adventures, and then you came along and there was a real one."

The afternoon flew by. Would there ever be enough time for all they wanted to say and hear?

But then Mrs. Granger, putting her finger to her lips, said quietly, "Shsh—someone's coming. I'm going to pretend," she had a mischievous look in her pale hazel eyes that reminded the girls so much of their friend, "that I'm asleep."

There was a brief knock and the door opened. A short, rather plain care assistant, whose mousy coloured hair was pulled tightly back from her forehead, entered the room. She wore a badge bearing the name Perdita Wells pinned to her chest. She had Reetta in tow. Holly stifled a giggle; she couldn't imagine anyone looking less like a Perdita.

Reetta brought in a tray bearing a covered white china plate and a small plastic dish containing a jelly, topped with an oversized dollop of cream. Unseen by Perdita, Mrs. Granger indicated the jelly with a slight movement of her finger and pulled a face at Holly and Beth. It was all they could do to stop themselves from laughing out loud.

"Come along now, Ada, time for supper," muttered Perdita.

Ada was her first name, but she'd never used it in all her life. Why couldn't they show some respect and address her as Mrs. Granger? But she gave no resistance as they busied themselves tucking a table napkin round her and pulling her up into a sitting position.

Perdita, unsmiling, pushed the bed tray in front of her.

"Come along now, you must eat up tonight. We can't have you starving yourself now, can we? You know how important it is to keep up your strength." She spoke harshly, without looking at the old lady.

It was too much for Beth. "You mustn't speak to my great-granny like that! She's my friend. We played together on the beach the day before yesterday, and I taught her my new dance steps. You just can't see her as she really is." She stormed to the window again, anger seething up in her.

Mrs. Granger spoke not a word, but Katy said quietly, "It's true. She did. But you wouldn't understand."

Her grandmother put her hand gently on Katy's arm and shook her head as if to say, "Don't say any more." Perdita and Reetta saw nothing of the movement. They glanced at each other, but to Katy they gave no reply.

"We'll be back with your evening drink later," said Perdita as they went out leaving the door ajar behind them. Katy promptly got up and shut it.

"Lucky old me," said the old lady with a chuckle as their footsteps died away down the corridor.

Holly said, "Oh Great-Granny! Why didn't you tell them? I hated it. I hated the way they spoke to you."

"I know, dear. I did, too. But, you see, as your mother said, they wouldn't understand, would they? Suppose they told Matron? Suppose she told the local newspaper, and I had my photograph all over the front of next week's Lower Gladon News and Mail? Then I might be asked for a television interview and goodness knows what would happen next."

Katy and the girls all burst our laughing at the pretend shocked look on the old lady's face.

"No, it's best kept to ourselves here. But I do wish the staff could see beyond our wrinkled faces and white hair and slow old bodies. We were all young once like they are, and inside we're just the same. But of course you know that, don't you, darlings?"

"Of course we do, Great-Granny!" said Holly. "We'll never forget our friend Marjorie. Do you know, we didn't even know your name was Marjorie, did we, Beth? We just always knew you as Great-Granny. You didn't really have a *name*."

"We won't ever, ever forget you, Great-Granny," said Beth, "or Amelia or Josh or Dulcie and Tallulah or—"

"Or Mia's brothers," put in Holly, "or Tallulah's sisters or…or—"

"Or Peter! Peter's so funny. He's such a clever dog. I've never seen a dog dance like that before." Beth had slipped easily into the present tense without noticing it. It just seemed natural.

The golden sunlight of the late afternoon had turned to a warm red glow in the west. The deepening blue sky was streaked with violet and green, and the first star had appeared: Venus, the evening star, a bright point of light in the blue.

"My dears, you must go," said Mrs. Granger. "You have a long journey home and an even longer one tomorrow. Thank you, oh thank you for coming. You have made me remember what it was like to be young again. Now, would you put that table lamp on for me, Beth? I want to remember all your faces clearly as they are now. Thank you, darling."

The book, which Beth had first seen in Amelia's hands, lay on the bedside table beside the lamp. She picked it up and opened it for one last look.

"Oh, Great-Granny, here are those strange words you said to Mummy when we came in!" She smoothed the page down with her hand and read carefully: 'How time is slipping underneath our feet. Unborn tomorrow and dead yesterday, why fret about them if today be sweet...' But yesterday's not dead, is it? We know that, don't we? I don't understand."

"I think the writer was trying to tell us we should be happy for today," said Mrs. Granger, "whenever that may be. We can't change the past, even if we're very blessed and for a brief moment we're able to slip into it like you two did, but it will always be part of us."

"Great-Granny," said Holly as she leaned over Beth's shoulder and slowly turned the pages, "this Omar Khyam guy; when did he write all this?" The words and pictures fascinated her.

"Oooh, about a thousand years ago."

"A thousand? *A thousand?*" said Holly. "That's really cool!"

Katy picked up her bag and jacket, not wanting to leave but knowing they had to, for it was getting very late. "Dearest Granny, please, please, take care of yourself," she said. "We'll come to see you when we get back."

The old lady's eyes had closed, but she nodded.

"You mustn't be worrying yourselves. Have a lovely time in France. I may be going away myself soon; a long holiday would do me good."

The questions and fears that leapt into all their thoughts were crushed before they could form into words by two beeps on Katy's mobile phone. She reached for her handbag.

"It's a text message," she said as she pressed 'Read'. "Here we are. It's from Mum and Dad. It says: 'Joshua born this a.m. 7 lbs 5 ozs. Rachel and baby both well. xxxx.' That's fantastic—it came just in time for us to tell you. Look!" Katy showed her grandmother the message.

"Joshua, another Josh." Her grandmother smiled as the girls cheered. "How lovely. Be sure to kiss the little one for me. Tell them about our adventures. All is well now. Do you know, we've travelled a long way today? And now..." she yawned and settled back into the moss-green armchair and closed her eyes again, "I'm rather sleepy. Au revoir, darlings. God Bless. Be sure now," her speech was becoming a little blurred and very quiet, "to give them all my love. Send them one of those..." She yawned again and pulled the rug a little higher. It was hard to make out her words, but the last thing they heard her say was, "Yes, send them one of those... those... telegram messages on your clever phone from me. It's good" she yawned again, "to have lived right into 2001. How the world has changed... how clever...."

§ § § § §

A moment later, she was asleep. Or was she? For surely, under the crocheted rug where her slippered feet could just be seen, there was movement, a slight tapping in time to some distant music coming from the direction of the town. There must have been a merry-go-round that had remained after the Steam Fair was over, for the music sounded for all the world like an old barrel organ.

20
Epilogue

The ferry pulled out of Dover Harbour exactly on time.

Holly and Beth had raced up several flights of steps from the car deck to watch as the big ship ploughed a furrow through the sea, leaving a foamy white wake stretching back towards the shore. How exciting it all was! The water was a long, long way down below them and looked so dark and rather scary, very different from the sea they knew, even from the end of the Palace Pier.

For a while, a flock of gulls followed, crying and swooping overhead, undaunted by the earsplitting blast from the funnel as the ship left port, but they soon tired of their games and were left far behind. The White Cliffs of Dover, so beloved of homecomers returning from foreign lands, gradually faded into the distance until they were nothing more than a hazy outline on the horizon.

It was a perfect day. The sky was a glorious clear blue, except for one unusual high, thin cloud. It could almost have been the vapour trail of an aeroplane had it been longer. The line of cloud crossed the sky just below the sun and tapered off in a little squiggle, making the sun look just like a big yellow balloon trailing its string in the wind.

§ § § § §

That night, Holly wrote a letter to her great-grandmother. It was found on Mrs. Granger's bedside table under her reading glasses on the day after she had left for that long rest she had promised herself. It lay beside a postcard from Beth, written in very small writing that ran across the card and up and down both sides and was surrounded by a row of xxxxs. The writing was so small that it was a little difficult to read, but the word 'dancing' appeared several times, and 'Peter' and something about 'fairies'. It ended 'with lots and lots and lots of love from ta amie in France, Beth. See you soon!' A p.s. had been added: 'I know you're not really an old lady' and more kisses.

Holly wrote:

Dearest Great-Granny Marjorie,

We've arrived safely at the campsite and it's very nice. Our tent is big and has two bedrooms and a sitting room. You'd like it here. There's a river and some mountains in the distance and a shop and a swimming pool. I can't wait it try it out! We went for a walk just after it got dark. There is a little wood near the river, and we saw hundreds and thousands of tiny flies that glowed. They were like tiny pinpricks of light. Mummy called them fireflies, but Daddy said they have another name which I can't remember. Beth called them fairy flies. I wish you could have seen them, it was magical!

We got home very quickly last night. Mum said we would. She said it was in record time.

The ferry was fun. We watched the White Cliffs of Dover until they were right out of sight. Beth wanted to pretend she was the heroine in 'Titanic' but we weren't allowed onto the bows of the ship. Did you see the film? I've just thought—you would have been six when the Titanic sank!

When we got to France we had to get the car off from the bottom deck which was hot and smelly and took ages, but Dad was okay and didn't get cross. He even let us put on my CD of Freddy and the Frisbees when we were driving away from Calais although he always hates it and says it's a horrible noise. Mummy went to sleep and so did Beth although she won't admit it. I think Dad secretly likes Freddy and the Frisbees because he was tapping his fingers on the steering wheel in time to the beat.

Tomorrow, I'm going to the shop to buy some stamps for this letter and the postcard Beth's writing to you, and I shall try out my French. I don't expect it's nearly as good as yours was at my age. I shall write 'Angleterre' on the envelope instead of England to make sure the French postmen get it to you quickly. I hope the English postmen understand.

I'm very, very sorry we never came to Wales. I wish we could have done. You could have taught Beth some Welsh dances, and I could have learned to play the harp and sing songs in Welsh. I wonder what Peter would have thought of that! I'll never, ever, ever forget our exciting adventure and the things we did together and I'm so, so glad that our friend Marjorie was you. I still can't really understand how it happened but we know it did, don't we, and if I start to think we dreamed it all, I can talk to Beth and Mummy and TO YOU and we can tell each other all over again what happened.

I do hope you get this letter all right. It would be just awful if you didn't because we never wrote to you in 1915, so I shall make a special wish when I post it that it will get to you quickly.

I shall have to stop now because it's getting dark and my torch battery's running out. It's very hot in the tent, and the crickets are making a lot of noise outside. I hope they don't get in because they might be tickly. I don't think they bite, though.

Mum says we'll be able to come and see you again when we get back. I do so hope we can. It will probably have to be a Saturday or Sunday because we go back to school the day after we get home. When we come I'll try to talk to you in French, and you'll be able to say how clever I am.

I hope you're having a nice rest and Reetta and Perdita have gone away and Matron's found some nicer nurses and you're not having to eat any more jelly because we know you don't like it.

With lots and lots of love, Au revoir, Holly xxxxx

p.s. I'll never, ever forget what Vera said on the beach about the war starting, like you never did. I'm thinking of telling Mrs. Howard (she's my science teacher) because she understands about time and stuff like that, but I'm not sure. What do you think?

p.p.s. Next term, I'm starting German! I know I shall think about Herr Munz, our German spy.

p.p.p.s. Beth brought one of her favourite books with her on holiday. It's called 'The House at Pooh Corner.' I expect you've read it. It was written ages and ages ago. Right at the end it says something about how Christopher Robin and Pooh will always be playing together in an enchanted place at the top of the forest. Maybe it's something like that with us and the beach hut.

p.p.p.p.s. Lots and Lots of love again, Holly. xxxxx"

Both the letter and the postcard were just a little crumpled, as if they had been read many times.